CW01511748

A Literary
Cat for
Every Day
of the Year

*For Luigi and Martha, the best cats
I have ever met.*

First published in Great Britain in 2025
by Cassell, an imprint of
Octopus Publishing Group Ltd
Carmelite House
50 Victoria Embankment
London EC4Y 0DZ
www.octopusbooks.co.uk

An Hachette UK Company
www.hachette.co.uk

The authorized representative in the EEA
is Hachette Ireland, 8 Castlecourt Centre,
Dublin 15, D15 XTP3, Ireland
(email: info@hbgi.ie)

Copyright © Octopus Publishing Group
2025

Distributed in the US by
Hachette Book Group
1290 Avenue of the Americas,
4th and 5th Floors
New York, NY 10104

Distributed in Canada by
Canadian Manda Group
664 Annette St., Toronto,
Ontario, Canada M6S 2C8

ISBN 978-0-7537-3566-4
eISBN 978-0-7537-3567-1

A CIP catalogue record for this book is
available from the British Library.

Printed and bound in Great Britain.

10 9 8 7 6 5 4 3 2 1

Publisher: Lucy Pessell
Senior Editor: Tim Leng
Designer: Isobel Platt
Illustrations: Isobel Platt
Assistant Editor: Samina Rahman
Production Controller: Sarah Parry

A Literary Cat for Every Day of the Year

Crafty companions and
mewling muses – the finest
felines in literature

Tara Richardson

C CASSELL

CONTENTS

INTRODUCTION

C ats and literature go together like tea and cake. It's not that you can't have one without the other, but there is a certain rightness to the pairing. Writers have chosen many animal companions over the years – often dogs, sometimes a raven (Charles Dickens) or, most oddly, a wombat (Dante Gabriel Rossetti) – but perhaps the most common is the cat. Whether stretching out at a writer's feet while they type or stalking imperiously across their desk as they try to work, tail twitching, there is something about cats that seems to draw in storytellers. Perhaps it's the way they seem to know things, with their steady green gazes and measured movements; perhaps it's the fact that they are able to amuse themselves, with none of the neediness we sometimes see in other creatures. And it's not just about providing company to writers – cats frequently feature in works of literature, whether they're the protagonists, the villains (Dragon, we're looking at you – see 11 January) or simply making a passing appearance, walking nonchalantly in and out of a scene with typical cattish disinterestedness. Their whiskered faces and knowing eyes appear in the pages of many a novel, poetry collection and memoir.

This book gathers together a selection of literary cats, from writer's companions to fictional felines, and presents you with a daily entry: the perfect way to bring more literature – and more cats – into your life.

After all, what could be better than more cats?

JANUARY

It's cold, it's dreary, payday is approximately 5,000 years away and your bank balance is looking distinctly meagre – but there is good news. Cats exist. And the best way to get through these dark, chilly winter days is to be as much like a cat as possible. Find a warm, cosy spot, ideally near a radiator (or, if you're very lucky, in a patch of wintry sun shining through the window). Curl up comfortably – and wait it out.

This month we'll be meeting one of the earliest recorded literary cats (see 7 January), along with Spider and Silver, the feline companions of two of the most celebrated writers of the last century. We'll also encounter no fewer than three witches' cats.

If the winter weeks feel too long and dreary, you might find yourself identifying with Pete, the cat featured in Robert A Heinlein's *The Door into Summer* (see 17 February and 8 June), who hates going outside when it's cold.

1 January

We start the New Year with the birthday of Eiko Kadono, author of *Kiki's Delivery Service* and creator of Jiji, the black cat who accompanies young witch Kiki as she embarks on a year of living alone as part of her witch's training. Perhaps now best known for inspiring the Studio Ghibli movie of the same name, the book is a thoughtful and charming meditation on growing up and friendship. The relationship at the heart of the novel is between Kiki and her feline pal Jiji, who stands by his friend through trials and tribulations, and even saves the day by heroically posing as a stuffed toy when the original goes missing. A fine cat to begin the year.

2 January

Today is sci-fi writer Isaac Asimov's birthday, and as such, it is often celebrated (unofficially) as Science Fiction Day. Asimov was a fan of felines, and famously switched his major from zoology to chemistry after being made to dissect a cat. He had a pet cat named Poky, and even wrote a short story about four-dimensional cats – called, ahem, 'Time Pussy'.

> Sure, the fourth dimension is time. These pussies was about a foot long and six inches wide and stretched somewhere into the middle o' next week. That's four dimensions, ain't it? Why, if you petted their heads, they wouldn't wag their tails till next day, mebbe. Some o' the big ones wouldn't wag till day after. Fact!

3 JANUARY

Today's cat is Tibby, one of the title characters of Doris Lessing's 'An Old Woman and Her Cat', a short story written for cold January days. It tells the tale of Hetty, an old woman who is 'not respectable'. After her husband dies and her children drift out of contact, Hetty finds a kitten and takes him in. He soon grows into 'a scarred warrior with fleas, a torn ear, and a ragged look to him' – but he's her constant companion, and the two adore each other. Tibby brings Hetty pigeons to cook when she's short of money, and she rewards him with saucers of milk and unlimited love. The two end up living in a derelict building after Hetty rejects the offer of being rehomed somewhere that won't accept Tibby too, and they huddle together in the 'sleety January weather'. It's a sad story about how easily vulnerable people can fall through the cracks and drift out of society, but it also highlights the unconditional love and loyalty between woman and cat.

4 January

Writer and Nobel Prize-winner Albert Camus died on this day in 1960. He loved cats, and is said to have had a pet cat named Cigarette. Here's a feline-focused quote from his existentialist novel, *A Happy Death*.

> The cats sleep for days at a time and make love from the first star until dawn. Their pleasures are fierce, and their sleep impenetrable. And they know that the body has a soul in which the soul has no part.

5 January

January is a time for self-reflection and new beginnings, which makes it a perfect moment to revisit *Aesop's Fables* – specifically those featuring felines. 'The Fox and the Cat' is a particular favourite; it tells of a fox and a cat who begin comparing notes on their skills. The fox boasts that it has many tricks up its furry sleeve, while the cat says it has only one: climbing trees. They are disturbed by the sound of hunters approaching. The cat quickly puts its one skill into practice and climbs to safety. The fox, unable to choose which of its many tricks to go for, hesitates too long and is caught.

You can just picture the cat nonchalantly licking its paw from the safety of the high branches. Take a leaf out of the cat's book: know yourself, your skills and your limits, and take decisive action when it matters.

6 January

I think all cats are wild cats. They just act tame if they
think they'll get a saucer of milk out of it.

– Douglas Adams and Mark Carwardine,
Last Chance to See

7 January

Continuing the theme of cats and milk (although it should be
said that feeding them milk is typically not advised), here are
a few lines from Geoffrey Chaucer's *The Canterbury Tales*. It
seems that even in the Middle Ages, cats could be relied upon
to do precisely as they wished, and nothing else.

Lets take a cat and foster him well with milk
And tender flesh, and make his couch of silk,
And lat him see a mouse go by the wall,
Anon he waiveth milk and flesh and all,
And every dainty that is in that house,
Such appetite hath he to eat a mouse.

– 'The Manciple's Tale', lines 175–180

8 January

'I love cats,' said Dorothy. 'They are so nice and selfish.
Dogs are TOO good and unselfish. They make me feel
uncomfortable. But cats are gloriously human.'

– L M Montgomery, *Anne of the Island*

9 JANUARY

Today marks the birthday of Barbara Sleigh, children's writer and creator of the one and only *Carbonel: The King of the Cats*. Stolen from his cradle as a kitten by a witch, he meets the young Rosemary when she buys him, along with the witch's broom, at a market.

> In the first place you thought you had bought a common witch's cat. Mind you, I'm not blaming you. A very natural mistake. You were not to know that I am a Royal Cat.

10 JANUARY

Cats, as a class, have never completely got over the snootiness caused by the fact that in Ancient Egypt they were worshipped as gods.

– P G Wodehouse, *Mulliner Nights*

11 January

Today marks the birthday of Robert C O'Brien, author of the thrilling children's book *Mrs Frisby and the Rats of NIMH*. With a mouse (Mrs Frisby) and highly intelligent rats as the protagonists, it's no surprise that the feline element in this book is considered a villain – but what a villain. Dragon the cat is owned by the farmer on whose land Mrs Frisby and her children live, and his reign of terror strikes fear into the hearts of all who encounter him.

> Dragon lay stretched out in the sunlight, but he was not asleep. His head was up and his yellow eyes were open, staring in her direction. [Mrs Frisby] gasped in terror and whirled around the fence post to put it between her and him. Then, without pausing, she set out on a dash across the garden as fast as she could run, expecting at any instant to hear the cat's scream and feel his great claws on her back.

12 January

Today is the birthday of one of the greatest cat fans in the literary world: Haruki Murakami, who even named a jazz club Peter Cat after one of his pets. So many of his works feature felines that he's likely to make more than one appearance in this book, but today let's turn our attention to *The Wind-up Bird Chronicle*, a meandering and beautiful tale that begins with the narrator, Toru Okada, setting out to find his missing cat.

> I had always liked cats. And I liked this particular cat. But cats have their own way of living. They're not stupid. If a cat stopped living where you happened to be, that meant it had decided to go somewhere else.

13 January

'If man could be crossed with the cat it would improve man, but it would deteriorate the cat.'

– Mark Twain

14 January

Today's cat is from the poem 'She sights a Bird – she chuckles' by American poet Emily Dickinson. As well as the feline featured below, Dickinson's copious letters frequently feature the family cats, as you'll see on later dates this year.

She sights a bird – she chuckles –
She flattens – then she crawls –
She runs without the look of feet –
Her eyes increase to Balls.

15 January

Peter Christen Asbjørnsen, writer and collector of Norwegian folklore, was born on this day in 1812. One of his stories is 'The Cat on the Dovrefjell', which features a traveller who has caught a white bear and is on his way to present it to the King of Denmark. One night he stops at a cottage and asks for shelter, but the owner tells him that it's not safe as it's Christmas Eve, the night the trolls come down from the mountain. The traveller begs, and the homeowner relents, leaving the house with his family and cat, and allowing the traveller and the bear to sleep there. The trolls come and mistake the bear for the cottager's cat, and it chases them from the cottage. The next year, the trolls return, but as they approach they call out to the cottager to ask if he still has his cat. Confused, he says yes – and now she has seven kittens, each even bigger than she. The trolls flee and never return.

16 JANUARY

Today's cat is Gobbolino from *Gobbolino the Witch's Cat* by Ursula Moray Williams, which was first published in January 1942. Unlike the other witch's cats, which have sleek black fur and green eyes, little Gobbolino has blue eyes and one white paw. As the kittens begin their training, Gobbolino struggles and is rejected by the witches. He sets out to fulfil his dream of becoming a kitchen cat instead, but his magic always seems to get in the way.

'I'll be a kitchen cat,' said Gobbolino. 'I'll sit by the fire with my paws tucked under my chest and sing like the kettle on the hob.'

❧

17 JANUARY

'Cats.'
'What about them?'
'They've got a parasite. Toxoplas-something.'
Nora knew this. She had known this since she was a teen, doing her work experience at Bedford Animal Rescue Centre. 'Toxoplasmosis.'
'That's it! Well, I was listening to this podcast, right… and there's this theory that this international group of billionaires infected the cats with it so that they could take over the world by making humans dumber and dumber. I mean, think about it. There are cats everywhere.'

– Matt Haig, *The Midnight Library*

18 JANUARY

Today marks the birthday of A A Milne, who was born on this day in 1882. Although Milne's best-known creation is of the ursine persuasion, one of Winnie-the-Pooh's closest buddies is Tigger, a big(ish) cat with a big personality. Tigger makes his first appearance in 1928's *The House at Pooh Corner*, and with his endless bouncing and high energy, he has become a firm favourite with fans of the Hundred-Acre Woods.

19 JANUARY

American novelist Patricia Highsmith was born on this day in 1921, and today's cat is her beloved pet Spider, to whom she dedicated her 1964 book *The Glass Cell*. When Highsmith moved from Italy to the UK, she couldn't bring Spider with her, and he was adopted by her friend and fellow writer Muriel Spark, meaning he lived with not one but two of the most famous writers of the twentieth century. Spark said of Spider: 'You could tell he had been a writer's cat. He would sit by me, seriously, as I wrote.'

20 JANUARY

The long, dark evenings of January are the perfect time to indulge in a little philosophizing. Perhaps this musing from the journals of Henry David Thoreau could get you started:

'What sort of philosophers are we, who know absolutely nothing of the origin and destiny of cats?'

21 JANUARY

Today's cat is Silver, the beloved pet of writer Jeanette Winterson. Winterson has described her first encounter with the tiny kitten – 'a small scrumble of tarnished silver fur with bright blue eyes' – who was given to her by the author of *The Woman in Black*, Susan Hill. The kitten had been taken from her mother at just five weeks. Winterson wrote, 'I am adopted, so I know what it is to leave your mother too soon.' (In fact, Winterson was adopted on this day in 1960.) Silver and Winterson soon became fast friends, and the cat kept her company during long writing sessions, occasionally 'helping' by tapping at the screen or trying to push buttons on the keyboard. Sadly, Silver is no longer with us, but one of her kittens was given to the novelist Ali Smith: a truly literary feline dynasty.

22 January

Poet, public figure and all-round scoundrel Lord Byron was born on this day in 1788. The writer was known to keep cats – although, as a letter written by his friend Percy Shelley reveals, he had a few other pets too...

Lord B.'s establishment consists, besides servants, of ten horses, eight enormous dogs, three monkeys, five cats, an eagle, a crow, and a falcon; and all these, except the horses, walk about the house, which every now and then resounds with their unarbitrated quarrels, as if they were the masters of it.

– Letters: Shelley in Italy

23 January

Today marks the birthday of poet Vernon Scannell. Although best known for his war poetry, Scannell also penned a rather dark piece about a cat. It opens:

> They should not have left him there alone,
> Alone that is except for the cat...
>
> – 'A Case of Murder'

And only grows more sinister from there. You've been warned!

24 January

In George R R Martin's A Song of Ice and Fire book series, the tough, no-nonsense Arya Stark is most commonly associated with wolves. But she does, on occasion, take on more of a feline identity, using the alias 'Cat' and trying to be more cat-like as she tries to survive the chaos of Braavos.

> Cats never weep, she told herself, no more than wolves. It's just a stupid dream.
>
> – *A Feast for Crows*

25 January

Today marks Virginia Woolf's birthday, so let's celebrate with some of the cat references in her iconic essay *A Room of One's Own*. Although a recurring feature in the essay is a rather morose-looking Manx cat, whose lack of tail seems to symbolize a general sense of loss ('I watched the Manx cat pause in the middle of the lawn as if it too questioned the universe, something seemed lacking, something seemed different'), it's hard to resist her razor-sharp takedown of an 'old gentleman' who doubted the writing prowess of women.

> [...] I thought of that old gentleman, who is dead now, but was a bishop, I think, who declared that it was impossible for any woman, past, present, or to come, to have the genius of Shakespeare. He wrote to the papers about it. He also told a lady who applied to him for information that cats do not as a matter of fact go to heaven, though they have, he added, souls of a sort. How much thinking those old gentlemen used to save one! How the borders of ignorance shrank back at their approach! Cats do not go to heaven. Women cannot write the plays of Shakespeare.

Woolf surely proved him wrong on the writing front – so let's assume it's safe to say he was wrong about cats and heaven, too.

26 January

On this day in 2000, author Kathleen Hale, creator of the Orlando the Marmalade Cat series of children's books, passed away. In her honour, today's cats are not just Orlando himself, but also his beautiful cat-wife Grace, a fashion icon whose outfits over the course of the books included a fetching full-length bathing suit complete with yellow swim hat, and a stunning gown adorned with prawn husks and a crown made of fish bones.

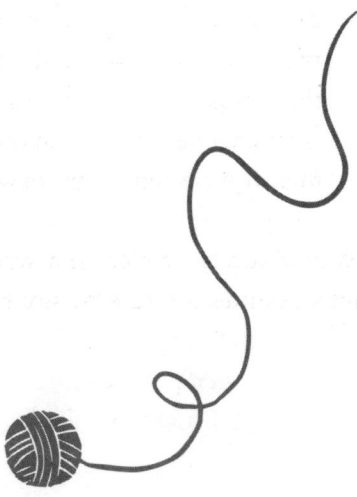

27 January

Today marks Lewis Carroll's birthday. Although no book on literary cats would be complete without at least a mention of the Cheshire Cat (and we'll get to him), today's cat is another feline favourite from *Alice's Adventures in Wonderland*: Dinah. Dinah is Alice's pet cat in the real world, and the first person she thinks of when she first begins her long fall down the rabbit hole into Wonderland.

Down, down, down. There was nothing else to do, so Alice soon began talking again. 'Dinah'll miss me very much to-night, I should think!' (Dinah was the cat.) 'I hope they'll remember her saucer of milk at tea-time. Dinah my dear! I wish you were down here with me! There are no mice in the air, I'm afraid, but you might catch a bat, and that's very like a mouse, you know. But do cats eat bats, I wonder?' And here Alice began to get rather sleepy, and went on saying to herself, in a dreamy sort of way, 'Do cats eat bats? Do cats eat bats?' and sometimes, 'Do bats eat cats?' for, you see, as she couldn't answer either question, it didn't much matter which way she put it. She felt that she was dozing off, and had just begun to dream that she was walking hand in hand with Dinah, and saying to her very earnestly, 'Now, Dinah, tell me the truth: did you ever eat a bat?' when suddenly, thump! thump! down she came upon a heap of sticks and dry leaves, and the fall was over.

28 January

On this day in 1873, Sidonie Gabrielle Colette – best known as simply Colette – was born. In her novel *Chance Acquaintances*, she neatly sums up the few possessions a woman needs:

> I went to collect the few personal belongings which…I held to be invaluable: my cat, my resolve to travel, and my solitude.

J D Salinger's *Franny and Zooey*, which tells the story of a brother trying to help his sister through an existential crisis, was initially published in two parts: as a short story, 'Franny', which was published on this day in 1955 in the *New Yorker*, and a novella, *Zooey*. Missing from the title of the combined book was today's cat, the charming (and perhaps rather grumpy) Bloomberg, who seems to act as a sort of conduit for the emotions the siblings struggle to express to each other.

Franny took [the cat] under the shoulders and lifted him up into intimate greeting distance. 'Good morning, Bloomberg dear!' she said, and kissed him fervently between the eyes. He blinked with aversion. 'Good morning, old fat smelly cat. Good morning, good morning, good morning!'

She gave him kiss after kiss, but no reciprocal waves of affection rose from him. He made an inept and rather violent attempt to cross over to Franny's collarbone. He was a very large mottled-gray 'altered' tomcat. 'Isn't he being affectionate?' Franny marvelled. 'I've never seen him so affectionate.'

30 January

Lloyd Alexander was born on this day in 1924. Among his many works is the novel *Time Cat*, about a cat – very pleasingly named Gareth – who can travel through time. As we come towards the end of this long, dark month, let's enjoy some wise words from *Time Cat*.

> The only thing a cat worries about is what's happening right now. As we tell the kittens, you can only wash one paw at a time.

31 January

Another Murakami quote to round out this month of cats, books and more cats:

> 'I like to read books. I like to listen to music. I collect records. And cats. I don't have any cats right now. But if I'm taking a walk and I see a cat, I'm happy.'
>
> – Haruki Murakami

FEBRUARY

With winter seeming to stretch out interminably, February can be a gloomy month, but hang in there. The days are getting incrementally longer, and the earliest flowers are beginning to push their way through the soil – namely the snowdrop, which incidentally is also the name of one of the kittens in Lewis Carroll's *Through the Looking-Glass* – see 22 September.

This month's cats play ping-pong (see 1 February), cure ailments (see 16 February), refuse to walk through doors despite demanding they be opened (see 17 and 26 February) and, of course, sleep (see 13 February).

Moveable feasts

CHINESE NEW YEAR: Chinese New Year begins on the new moon between 21 January and 20 February. Each year is assigned an animal according to the Chinese zodiac, and these repeat in a twelve-year cycle. The Vietnamese zodiac is similar, with a few key differences – one of which is that when the Chinese zodiac marks the Year of the Rabbit, the Vietnamese version celebrates the Year of the Cat.

1 FEBRUARY

Legendary writer Muriel Spark was born on this day in 1918. To mark her birthday, today's cat is the ping-pong-playing Bluebell from her novel *Robinson*.

[...] I began daily to play with [Bluebell], sometimes throwing the ping-pong ball in the air. She often leapt beautifully and caught it in her forepaws. By the second week in June I had so far won her confidence and approval as to be able to make fierce growling noises at her. She liked these very much, and would crouch menacingly before me, springing suddenly at me in mock attack.

2 February

Charles Dickens's *Oliver Twist* was, like many of his works, published in serial format. The first part of this book came out in February 1837. Although the animal with the biggest role in the novel is undoubtedly Bill Sikes's terrier Bulls-eye, we are treated to a brief and very pleasing glimpse of some cats in the interaction below between the rather pompous Mr Bumble and the object of his affections, Mrs Corney.

'You have a cat, ma'am, I see,' said Mr. Bumble, glancing at one who, in the centre of her family, was basking before the fire; 'and kittens too, I declare!'

'I am so fond of them, Mr. Bumble, you can't think,' replied the matron. 'They're so happy, so frolicsome, and so cheerful, that they are quite companions for me.'

'Very nice animals, ma'am,' replied Mr. Bumble, approvingly; 'so very domestic.'

'Oh, yes!' rejoined the matron with enthusiasm; 'so fond of their home too, that it's quite a pleasure, I'm sure.'

'Mrs. Corney, ma'am,' said Mr. Bumble, slowly, and marking the time with his teaspoon, 'I mean to say this, ma'am; that any cat, or kitten, that could live with you, ma'am, and not be fond of its home, must be a ass, ma'am.'

3 FEBRUARY

Today's cat is more of an idea than a character; a rule, if you will. *Ancrene Wisse* was a handbook thought to have been written by a priest in the early 13th century for three sisters who wanted to become anchoresses (religious women who shut themselves away to live a life of quiet contemplation). As well as covering their daily routines, and rules for what they should wear, eat and drink, the book explains that 'ne schule ye habben nan beast bute cat ane', which means, 'you should not keep any animals, except a single cat'.

4 FEBRUARY

Today's cat is the central figure in the poem 'A 14 year old convalescent cat in winter', written by Gavin Ewart, who was born on this day in 1916. Describing a well-loved pet, the poet notes 'I want him to have another living summer', describing how the sweet old cat might stretch out in the sun once more.

5 February

Writer William S Burroughs was born on this day in 1914. As well as writing eighteen novels and being considered a key figure in the Beat movement, he was also a dedicated cat-lover, as all good writers should be.

The cat does not offer services. The cat offers itself. Of course he wants care and shelter. You don't buy love for nothing. Like all pure creatures, cats are practical.

– *The Cat Inside*

6 February

Today's cat is Topsy, beloved pet of one Milly-Molly-Mandy, star of a series of children's books written by Joyce Lankester Brisley (who was born on this day in 1896).

When bedtime drew near, they had their baths [...]. And then Milly-Molly-Mandy in her red dressing gown, and little-friend-Susan in Grandma's red shawl, sat in front of the fire on little stools (with Toby the dog on one side, and Topsy the cat on the other).

– *Milly-Molly-Mandy Stories*

7 February

Victorian author Charles Dickens was born on this day in 1812. Cats pop up in several of his works (see 2 February, 1 May and 12 September), but today's cat is not fictional. Bob was one of a litter born to Dickens's daughter's cat Williamina. Although the rest were given away, Bob stuck around, and became known to the household servants as 'the master's cat' due to his devotion to Dickens. And it seems the devotion was returned; when Bob passed away, Dickens had his paw preserved and made into the handle for a paper knife.

8 February

American poet Elizabeth Bishop was born on this day in 1911. In her honour, today's cat is Minnow, the subject of her poem 'Lullaby for the Cat'.

Darling Minnow, drop that frown,
Just cooperate.
Not a kitten shall be drowned
In the Marxist state!

9 FEBRUARY

Today marks the birthday of writer Alice Walker, author of *The Color Purple*. As well as her remarkable writing and tireless work as a social activist, Walker is known for her love of cats, including her beloved pets Tuscaloosa and Frida (named for Frida Kahlo).

10 FEBRUARY

Everything a cat is and does physically is to me beautiful, lovely, stimulating, soothing, attractive and an enchantment.

– Paul Gallico, *Honorable Cat*

11 FEBRUARY

Today's cat is Kitsa, the family pet in Lynne Reid Banks's children's novel series The Indian in the Cupboard, about a young boy named Omri and a magical cupboard that he discovers can bring plastic figurines to life.

[Omri's] black-and-white cat, Kitsa, was sitting on the draining board. She watched him out of her knowing green eyes as he came to get a drink of water.

'You're not supposed to be up there, Kits,' he said. 'You know that.' She continued to stare at him. [...] He laughed and stroked her head. He was crazy about her. He loved her independence and disobedience.

– *Return of the Indian*

12 February

American author Judy Blume was born on this day in 1938.
Beloved for her children's and young-adult novels, including
Are You There God? It's Me, Margaret, Blume is an animal-
lover and owned a calico cat that lived to the age of sixteen.
Her 1977 novel *Starring Sally J. Freedman as Herself* features
a cat named Omar:

> The Rubins had an all-white cat, called Omar, who slept
> under the covers with Andrea. He was the most beautiful
> cat Sally had ever seen but Mom said, 'He may be very
> pretty but cats can be full of worms so watch out…no
> use looking for trouble.'

13 February

Children's writer Eleanor Farjeon was born on this day in
1881. To mark the occasion, here are a few lines of her playful
poem about the snoozing habits of cats.

> Cats sleep, anywhere,
> Any table, any chair,
> Top of piano, window-ledge
> In the middle, on the edge.

– 'Cats'

14 FEBRUARY

Today is Valentine's Day, so enjoy these musings on love from the writer Charles Bukowski. (We'll be hearing more from this famous cat-lover as the year goes on.)

'I don't like love as a command, as a search, it must come to you, like a hungry cat at the door.'
– *Screams from the Balcony: Selected Letters 1960–1970*

15 FEBRUARY

Today's cat is Puck, one of the kittens in Kathi Appelt's children's book *The Underneath*, the story of an abandoned cat, her kittens (Puck and Sabine) and a poorly treated dog named Ranger. They all live together underneath the porch of a house – until the curious Puck wanders away from the safety of the porch and becomes lost.

Cats are built for naps, and Puck was no exception. He spent a lot of time snoozing. In between, he worked on his hunting skills. [...] With his belly full of a juicy mouse, he thought [Sabine] might be just a little proud of him. [...] For the first time in many days, he purred.
Purring is not so different from praying. To a tree, a cat's purr is one of the purest of all prayers, for in it lies a whole mixture of gratitude and longing, the twin ingredients of every prayer. Here then is a small cat, purring, praying that he will find his way to his sister and Ranger.'

16 FEBRUARY

Japanese author Syou Ishida clearly believes in the magic of cats: her novel *We'll Prescribe You a Cat* is centred around the Nakagyō Clinic for the Soul, where patients share their woes and are then prescribed a cat as treatment.

> They're very effective. You know the old saying: 'A cat a day keeps the doctor away.' Cats are more effective than any other medicine out there.

17 FEBRUARY

We'll be hearing more about cat-loving sci-fi writer Robert A Heinlein on 7 July, but for now, please enjoy his thoughts on something all cat-owners can relate to: having to constantly open doors for our tiny feline masters. The extract below is from Heinlein's novel *The Door into Summer*. (See 26 February for more literary mutterings on cats and doors.)

> I have spent too much of my life opening doors for cats – I once calculated that, since the dawn of civilization, nine hundred and seventy-eight man-centuries have been used up that way. I could show you figures.

18 FEBRUARY

American journalist Helen Rowland was known for her humorous column 'Reflections of a Bachelor Girl', which was published in *The New York World*. You could think of her as a sort of early-twentieth-century Carrie Bradshaw. Although her specialist subject was men, she occasionally made use of felines in her comparisons. Here are a few gems.

'Flinging yourself at a man's head is like flinging a bone at a cat; it doesn't fascinate him, it frightens him.'

'A man is like a cat; chase him and he'll run; sit still and ignore him and he'll come purring at your feet.'

'Appealing to a man's sense of humour when he has just lathered his face for shaving, is about as effective as appealing to a cat's sense of honour when she sees a chance to steal the milk.'

19 FEBRUARY

When she wasn't writing poetry (see 14 January), Emily Dickinson was a dedicated writer of letters. Below, she shares the sad news of the death of a family cat – and her response to it.

Vinnie is deeply affected in the death of her dappled cat, though I convince her it is immortal, which assists her some.

– Emily Dickinson, letter to Mrs J G Holland, 1857

20 FEBRUARY

She is a grey cat, but around their eyes the fur is black,
so that she looks a little like those fifteen-year-olds who
believe that being Cleopatra is mostly a matter of mascara.

– Jessamyn West, *A Matter of Time*

21 FEBRUARY

Today marks the birth in 1635 of Thomas Flatman, English
poet and miniature painter (that is to say, he painted miniature
portraits – he wasn't particularly small himself). Here is his
poem 'An Appeal to Cats in the Business of Love'.

Ye cats at midnight spit love at each other,
Who best feel the pangs of a passionate lover,
I appeal to your scratches and your tattered fur,
If the business of Love be no more than to purr.
Old Lady Grimalkin with her gooseberry eyes,
Knew something when a kitten, for why she is wise;
You find by experience, the love-fit's soon o'er,
Puss! Puss! lasts not long, but turns to Cat-whore!
Men ride many miles
Cats tread many tiles
Both hazard their necks in the fray;
Only cats when they fall
From a house or a wall,
Keep their feet, mount their tails, and away!

22 FEBRUARY

Artist and writer Edward Gorey was born on this day in 1925. His iconic drawings are instantly recognisable, and many cat-lovers will know him as the illustrator of T S Eliot's *Old Possum's Book of Practical Cats* (which we will be revisiting as the year goes on). Below are a couple of answers he gave to *Vanity Fair*'s 'Proust Questionnaire' back in 1997.

What or who is the greatest love of your life?
    Cats.

If you could change one thing about your family, what would it be?
    To live with cats who are a tad less loopy.

23 February

English Romantic poet John Keats died on this day in 1821. He might be best known for 'Ode to a Nightingale', but he also penned a few lines about a feline friend in his poem 'Sonnet To Mrs Reynold's Cat':

Cat! who hast pass'd thy grand climacteric,
How many mice and rats hast in thy days
Destroy'd? How many tit bits stolen? Gaze
With those bright languid segments green, and prick
Those velvet ears – but pr'ythee do not stick
Thy latent talons in me -- and upraise
Thy gentle mew – and tell me all thy frays,
Of fish and mice, and rats and tender chick.
Nay, look not down, nor lick thy dainty wrists--
For all thy wheezy asthma – and for all
Thy tail's tip is nick'd off – and though the fists
Of many a maid have given thee many a maul,
Still is that fur as soft, as when the lists
In youth thou enter'dest on glass bottled wall.

24 FEBRUARY

Gone Girl author Gillian Flynn was born on this day in 1971.

Sleep is like a cat. It only comes to you if you ignore it.
– Gone Girl

25 FEBRUARY

She's a cat with a strong sense of order and the rightness of things, and would have made an excellent secretary.
– Barbara Holland, The Secrets of the Cat

26 FEBRUARY

French author Victor Hugo was born on this day in 1802. As this quote from his epic *Les Misérables* shows, even the world's most famous writers can't make a cat walk through a door unless it wants to.

Every one has noticed the taste which cats have for pausing and lounging between the two leaves of a half-shut door. Who is there who has not said to a cat, 'Do come in!' There are men who, when an incident stands half-open before them, have the same tendency to halt in indecision between two resolutions, at the risk of getting crushed through the abrupt closing of the adventure by fate. The over-prudent, cats as they are, and because they are cats, sometimes incur more danger than the audacious. Fauchelevent was of this hesitating nature.

27 February

American author John Steinbeck was born on this day in 1902. He is perhaps best known for his seminal works *The Grapes of Wrath* and *Of Mice and Men*, but today's cat is from his 1961 work *The Winter of our Discontent*.

For the first time in my memory, I went into the alley with pleasure and opened the back door with excitement. The cat was by the door, waiting. I can't remember a morning when that lean and efficient cat hasn't been waiting to try to get in the back door and I have never failed to throw a stick at him or run him off. To the best of my knowledge, he has never got in. I call the cat 'he' because his ears are torn up from fighting. Are cats strange animals or do they so resemble us that we find them curious as we do monkeys? Perhaps six or eight hundred times that cat has tried to get in and he has never made it.

28 FEBRUARY

French philosopher Michel de Montaigne was born on this day in 1533, and was one of the key thinkers (and essay-writers) of the Renaissance. Here, he ponders the idea of presumption, trying to consider his cat's perspective:

Presumption is our natural and original disease. The most wretched and frail of all creatures is man, and withal the proudest. [...] [He] equals himself to God, attributes to himself divine qualities, withdraws and separates himself from the crowd of other creatures, cuts out the shares of the animals, his fellows and companions, and distributes to them portions of faculties and force, as himself thinks fit How does he know, by the strength of his understanding, the secret and internal motions of animals?—from what comparison betwixt them and us does he conclude the stupidity he attributes to them? When I play with my cat who knows whether I do not make her more sport than she makes me? We mutually divert one another with our play.

– *The Essays of Michel de Montaigne*

29 FEBRUARY

British author Derek Tangye was born on this day in 1912. He is known for his collection *The Minack Chronicles*, in which he recorded the details of his life living on a Cornish daffodil farm with his wife. Today's cat is their beloved pet Monty (named after General Montgomery), a ginger tomcat who appears in several of the books (and to whom one book, *A Cat in the Window*, is dedicated). Fittingly enough, considering that today is Leap Day, Tangye also wrote a book called *Monty's Leap*, referring to Monty's habit of jumping across a small stream near their home.

How do you summon up courage to dismiss a cat who is paying you the compliment of sitting in your lap?

The answer is simple: you don't.

MARCH

S pring is finally making an appearance, and you may notice your garden filling up with birds once more (if you have a cat, they've definitely noticed). Warmer weather and longer days are just around the corner.

March's cats are mad (see 1 March), mischievous (see 12 March) and murderous (see 5 March), yet resourceful and brave (see 13 March).

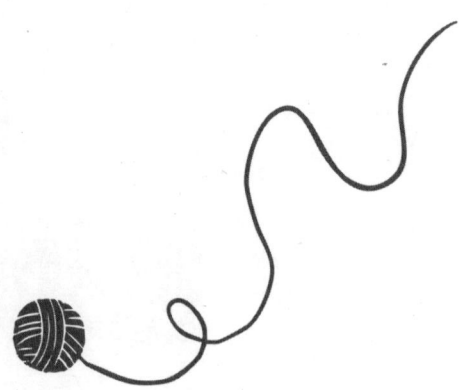

Moveable feasts

WORLD BOOK DAY: World Book Day is marked on the first Thursday in March. Many people choose to dress up as their favourite fictional characters to celebrate their love of reading. Why not don a pair of cat ears and some fancy footwear à la Puss in Boots (see 7 May)?

MOTHER'S DAY: In the UK, Mother's Day is celebrated on the fourth Sunday of Lent, meaning it usually falls in March or April (in the US, however, it is marked on the second Sunday in May). If you're looking for examples of feline mothers in literature, you can't go wrong with Lewis Carroll's Dinah (see 27 January and 22 April), or the long-suffering Tabitha Twitchit of Beatrix Potter fame (see 28 July).

1 March

When it comes to literary characters, it's hard to enter this month without thinking of Wonderland's longest-eared resident, the March Hare. But Alice would never have met him if it wasn't for the guidance of the Cheshire Cat.

The Cat only grinned when it saw Alice. It looked good-natured, she thought: still it had very long claws and a great many teeth, so she felt that it ought to be treated with respect.

'Cheshire Puss,' she began, rather timidly, as she did not at all know whether it would like the name: however, it only grinned a little wider. 'Come, it's pleased so far,' thought Alice, and she went on. 'Would you tell me, please, which way I ought to go from here?'

'That depends a good deal on where you want to get to,' said the Cat.

'I don't much care where—' said Alice.

'Then it doesn't matter which way you go,' said the Cat.

'—so long as I get somewhere,' Alice added as an explanation.

'Oh, you're sure to do that,' said the Cat, 'if you only walk long enough.'

Alice felt that this could not be denied, so she tried another question. 'What sort of people live about here?'

'In that direction,' the Cat said, waving its right paw round, 'lives a Hatter: and in that direction,' waving the other paw, 'lives a March Hare. Visit either you like: they're both mad.'

'But I don't want to go among mad people,' Alice remarked.

'Oh, you can't help that,' said the Cat: 'we're all mad here. I'm mad. You're mad.'

'How do you know I'm mad?' said Alice.

'You must be,' said the Cat, 'or you wouldn't have come here.'

Alice didn't think that proved it at all; however, she went on 'And how do you know that you're mad?'

'To begin with,' said the Cat, 'a dog's not mad. You grant that?'

'I suppose so,' said Alice.

'Well, then,' the Cat went on, 'you see, a dog growls when it's angry, and wags its tail when it's pleased. Now I growl when I'm pleased, and wag my tail when I'm angry. Therefore I'm mad.'

'I call it purring, not growling,' said Alice.

'Call it what you like,' said the Cat. 'Do you play croquet with the Queen to-day?'

'I should like it very much,' said Alice, 'but I haven't been invited yet.'

'You'll see me there,' said the Cat, and vanished.

Alice was not much surprised at this, she was getting so used to queer things happening. While she was looking at the place where it had been, it suddenly appeared again.

'By-the-bye, what became of the baby?' said the Cat. 'I'd nearly forgotten to ask.'

'It turned into a pig,' Alice quietly said, just as if it had come back in a natural way.

'I thought it would,' said the Cat, and vanished again '

– Lewis Carroll, *Alice's Adventures in Wonderland*

2 MARCH

Science-fiction novelist Philip K Dick, perhaps best known for his works *Do Androids Dream of Electric Sheep?* and *A Scanner Darkly* died on this day in 1982. In his honour, today's cat is his pet Magnificat, whom he mentioned in a 1953 interview with *Imagination* magazine. Dick was buried in Fort Morgan, Colorado, and there is an image of a cat on his gravestone.

3 MARCH

Today is International Writer's Day. As the entries in this book will no doubt make abundantly clear, many writers have feline companions, and depend on them for company and comfort during the long hours spent at a desk. While for some cats can be a welcome distraction when staring down a blank page, other writers feel their cats actively help them with getting words down – as Joyce Carol Oates reportedly told an audience at Boston Book Festival in 2010.

'I write so much because my cat sits on my lap. She purrs so I don't want to get up. She's so much more calming than my husband.'

4 MARCH

[F]or some years, my life did not include extras, unnecessaries, adornments. Cats had no place in an existence always spent moving from place to place, room to room. A cat needs a place as much as it needs a person to make its own.

– Doris Lessing, *Particularly Cats*

5 MARCH

Today's cat is Ming, the feline hero of the short story 'Ming's Biggest Prey' by Patricia Highsmith, whom we first met on 19 January. It tells the story of Ming the cat, and the revenge he takes on his mistress's cruel new boyfriend, Teddie.

People! Ming detested people. In all the world, he liked only Elaine. Elaine loved him and understood him.
    Especially this man called Teddie Ming detested now. [...] Ming did not like the way Teddie looked at him, when Elaine was not watching.

6 MARCH

American writer and journalist Ring Lardner, known for his satirical columns and love of baseball, was born on this day in 1885. Today's cats are Barney, Blackie and Ringer, his family's kittens and stars of a column in which he jokes that, although 'these 3 little members of the feline tribe is the cutest and best behaved kitties in all catdom' they might not have long to live, as he's been told that 'no finer or more warmer garment can be fashioned than is made from the skin of a milkfed kitty'. Happily, the Lardner kittens were spared – after all, 'the fur of 3 kittens would make a mighty small coat'.

7 MARCH

'The Boy Who Drew Cats' is a Japanese fairytale translated into English by Lafcadio Hearn. It tells the story of a young boy who is taken on as an acolyte by an elderly priest. But the boy has a fault: 'He liked to draw cats during study-hours, and to draw cats even where cats ought not to have been drawn at all.' Eventually he is sent away from the temple, so he sets off to seek out another temple where he might be accepted. He finds a large temple that is rumoured to have been abandoned due to the presence of an evil goblin creature. He spends the night there, drawing cats for comfort before he falls asleep. When he awakes next morning, he discovers the goblin – a rat-like creature – has been slain, and all his cat drawings now have mouths red with blood.

8 March

Novelist and writer of children's books Lore Segal was born on this day in 1928. To celebrate her birthday, today's cat is Purrly (later renamed Purrless), star of her children's book *The Story of Mrs Lovewright and Purrless Her Cat*. In this tale, Mrs Lovewright seeks out a pet cat in order to help her stay warm, but also for the pleasure of hearing it purr. Unfortunately, the cat she ends up with is not a purrer – but they find their way in the end.

9 March

Today's cat is the delightfully named Ian, who appears in Steven Hall's 2007 novel *The Raw Shark Texts* and manages to steal just about every scene in which he features.

At 3.30 p.m. on the second day of my second life, a big ginger tomcat arrived in the kitchen. He hauled his heavy self in through the open window, stepped across the worktops and planted himself down solid in the middle of the floor. Then he just sat there, staring up at me with round cynical eyes. I stared back, surprised. I thought he might run if I tried to get too close but he didn't budge at all, he just kept looking at me as I knelt down to read his collar tag. There was a name – Hello! I'm Ian – and a full address, although the first line told me everything I needed to know.

I had a housemate.

10 MARCH

'The poet is a man who lives at last by watching his moods. An old poet comes at last to watch his moods as narrowly as a cat does a mouse.'

– Henry David Thoreau

❧

11 MARCH

Today's cat is Lily, who finds herself in the midst of a complex love triangle in the novella *A Cat, A Man, and Two Women* by Juni'chirō Tanizaki. In the book, Shozo finds himself challenged for custody of Lily by his ex-wife, Shinako – but it soon becomes clear that each character is trying to use Lily as a pawn in their own game.

Considering all I've sacrificed, is it too much to ask for one little cat in return?

❧

12 MARCH

Today's cat is none other than The Cat in the Hat, star of the 1957 Dr Seuss book of the same name. Which of us, as a child, didn't secretly wish for this mischievous creature to show up and liven up a rainy day at home?

13 MARCH

American writer Mary Eleanor Wilkins Freeman died on this day in 1930. In her honour, today's feline is the unnamed cat from her short story 'The Cat', an independent yet loving creature who is left alone in a cabin over the winter and has to fend for himself. During the course of the long, cold months, a wanderer enters the cabin, half-dead from hunger and exhaustion, and the Cat goes hunting and shares his food with the starving man.

The snow was falling, and the Cat's fur was stiffly pointed with it, but he was imperturbable. He sat crouched, ready for the death-spring, as he had sat for hours. It was night— but that made no difference—all times were as one to the Cat when he was in wait for prey. Then, too, he was under no constraint of human will, for he was living alone that winter. Nowhere in the world was any voice calling him; on no hearth was there a waiting dish. He was quite free except for his own desires, which tyrannized over him when unsatisfied as now. The Cat was very hungry— almost famished, in fact. For days the weather had been very bitter, and all the feebler wild things which were his prey by inheritance, the born serfs to his family, had kept, for the most part, in their burrows and nests, and the Cat's long hunt had availed him nothing. But he waited with the inconceivable patience and persistency of his race; besides, he was certain. The Cat was a creature of absolute convictions, and his faith in his deductions never wavered. The rabbit had gone in there between those low-hung pine boughs. Now her little doorway had before it a shaggy curtain of snow, but in there she was. The Cat had seen her enter, so like a swift grey shadow that even his sharp and practised eyes had glanced back for the substance following, and then she was gone. So he sat down and waited, and he waited still in the whitenight, listening angrily to the north wind starting in the upper heights of the mountains with distant screams, then swelling into an awful crescendo of rage, and swooping down with furious white wings of snow like a flock of fierce eagles into the valleys and ravines. The Cat was on the side of a mountain, on a wooded terrace. Above him a few feet away towered the rock ascent as steep as the wall of a cathedral. The Cat had never climbed it—trees were the ladders to his heights of life. He had often looked with wonder at the rock, and miauled bitterly and resentfully as man does in the face of a forbidding Providence. At his left was the sheer precipice. Behind him, with a short stretch of woody growth between, was the frozen perpendicular wall of a mountain stream. Before him was the way to his home. When the rabbit came out she was trapped; her little cloven feet could not scale such unbroken steeps. So the Cat waited. [...] And now over all this whirl of wood and rock and dead trunks and branches and vines descended the snow. It blew down like smoke over the rock-crest above; it stood in a gyrating column like some death-wraith of nature, on the level, then it broke over the edge of the precipice, and the Cat cowered before the fierce backward set of it. It was as if ice needles pricked his skin through his beautiful thick fur, but he never faltered and never once cried. He had nothing to gain from crying, and everything to lose; the rabbit would hear him cry and know he was waiting.

14 MARCH

Poet and founder of the Poetry Bookshop Harold Monro was born on this day in 1879. Here are a few lines from his charming poem 'Milk for the Cat'.

The children eat and wriggle and laugh;
The two old ladies stroke their silk:
But the cat is grown small and thin with desire,
Transformed to a creeping lust for milk.

The white saucer like some full moon descends
At last from the clouds of the table above;
She sighs and dreams and thrills and glows,
Transfigured with love.

She nestles over the shining rim,
Buries her chin in the creamy sea;
Her tail hangs loose; each drowsy paw
Is doubled under each bending knee.

15 MARCH

Today is the birthday of James Bowen, who was born in 1979. Bowen is the author of *A Street Cat Named Bob*, which tells the story of how he met a cat (the eponymous Bob) who joined him while he was busking and ultimately inspired him to change his life.

My back was turned to the crowd when I again heard the distinctive clinking of one coin hitting another. Behind me I heard a male voice. 'Nice cat, mate,' he said.

I turned and saw an ordinary-looking guy in his mid-twenties giving me a thumbs-up sign and walking off with a smile on his face.

I was taken aback. Bob had curled himself up in a comfortable ball in the middle of the empty guitar case. I knew he was a charmer, but this was something else.

16 March

Everyone's favourite writer of witches, Alice Hoffman, was born on this day in 1952. She is perhaps best known for her beloved 1995 novel *Practical Magic*, which tells the story of sisters Sally and Gillian growing up with their aunts, whom everyone in the town suspects are witches. The passage below depicts young Sally attending school one day, without realizing that a troupe of her aunts' cats have followed her.

On this morning, Sally didn't even know the cats were behind her, until she sat down at her desk. Some of her classmates were laughing, but three girls had jumped up onto the radiator and were shrieking. Anyone would have thought a gang of demons had entered the room, but it was only those flea-bitten creatures that had followed Sally to school. They paraded past chairs and desks, black as night and howling like banshees.

17 March

In honour of St Patrick's Day, today's cat is Pangur Bán (or White Pangur), the companion of an Irish monk who wrote a poem about him in about the 9th century. Centuries later, he remains a very well-loved literary cat.

I and Pangur Bán, my cat,
'Tis a like task we are at;
Hunting mice is his delight,
Hunting words I sit at night.

18 March

Catriona Ward's chilling and mind-bending novel *The Last House on Needless Street* was published on this day in 2021. It tells the story of a strange, boarded-up house, and the cast of characters who reside there: the lonely Ted, his daughter Lauren and Olivia the cat. But as the narrative swoops and unfurls, the reader begins to realize that nothing is as it seems.

The cat sits back on her haunches and looks steadily at Dee. She is thin and ragged, ears torn from fighting. Her eyes are a soft tawny brown. Dee would not call her a beautiful cat. But she is a survivor.

The tabby puts her head on one side and makes an interrogative pprrrrp?

[…] Dee knows that her sister has not come back to her as a mangy alley cat. Of course not. That would be crazy. But she can't help the feeling that the cat pulled her out of the dream. That it is helping her, somehow.

19 MARCH

Stephen King's short story collection *Everything's Eventual* was published on this day in 2002. It includes the story 'L. T.'s Theory of Pets', in which the narrator blames the breakdown of his marriage on the family pets, a dog named Frank and a cat named Lucy – or sometimes Screwlucy.

> Cats are different, though. A cat won't curry favour even if it's in their best interests to do so. A cat can't be a hypocrite. If more preachers were like cats, this would be a religious country again. If a cat likes you, you know. If she doesn't, you know that, too. Screwlucy never liked Lulu, not one whit, and she made it clear from the start.

20 MARCH

Today's cat is Galanthis, and she wasn't initially a cat at all. In Greek mythology, Galanthis started out as the servant of Alcmene, best known as the mother of Heracles. While Alcmene was in labour with Heracles, the goddess Hera interfered, due to a longstanding feud with Zeus, Hera's unfaithful husband – and father of Heracles. When Galanthis realized what was happening, she played a trick to help Alcmene give birth, and in punishment, Hera turned her into a cat. (In some versions of the story, Galanthis is turned into a weasel, but of course we are sticking with the cat version here.)

21 MARCH

Today is World Poetry Day, and so our chosen (big) cat is from what must be one of the most famous poems featuring felines, 'The Tyger' by William Blake.

Tyger, tyger, burning bright
In the forests of the night,
What immortal hand or eye
Could frame thy fearful symmetry?

In what distant deeps or skies
Burnt the fire of thine eyes?
On what wings dare he aspire?
What the hand dare seize the fire?

And what shoulder and what art
Could twist the sinews of thy heart?
And, when thy heart began to beat,
What dread hand and what dread feet?

22 March

Today's cat is Punch, the purring companion of the agoraphobic protagonist in A J Finn's bestselling 2018 psychological thriller, *The Woman in the Window*.

Punch bounds onto the island between us and drops something from his mouth. I look at it.

A dead rat.

I recoil. I'm gratified to see that David does, too. It's a small one, with oil fur and a black worm of a tail; its body has been mauled.

Punch watches us proudly.

'No,' I scold him. He cocks his head.

'He really did a number on it,' David says.

23 March

'What is the cat?' he exclaimed. 'It's a correction. The good Lord, having made the mouse, said, 'Oh dear, that was a mistake!' And he made the cat. The cat is the mouse's erratum. The mouse, plus the cat, is the revised and corrected proof of creation.'

– Victor Hugo, *Les Misérables*

24 MARCH

Wise words on creating (and cat care) from Ray Bradbury.

> That's the great secret of creativity. You treat ideas like
> cats: you make them follow you.
>
> *– Zen in the Art of Writing*

25 MARCH

American writer and feminist activist Gloria Steinem was
born on this day in 1934. She is a known cat-lover, and her
feline companions have included Crazy Alice, Magritte and
Fendi. She is quoted as describing cats as 'a writer's most
logical and agreeable companion'. Couldn't agree more.

On this day in 1911, Thomas Lanier Williams was born – better known by his later pen name Tennessee Williams. Cat-lovers may be dismayed to discover that the 'cat' in his play *Cat on a Hot Tin Roof* is not a cat at all, but a woman named Maggie who sometimes refers to herself as 'Maggie the cat' due to her supposedly feline ways – she is cunning and can be manipulative, yet also has grace and strength.

MAE:
Maggie?
[Margaret turns with a smile.]
Why are you so catty?

MARGARET:
Cause I'm a cat! But why can't you take a joke, Sister Woman?

Metaphorical cats aside, Williams is said to have had a real-life cat named Sabbath.

27 March

Today is World Theatre Day, so we'll continue with yesterday's theatrical theme, while adding a nautical touch with Gilbert and Sullivan's *H.M.S. Pinafore*. In the excerpt below from Act II, Josephine and Ralph are attempting to secretly elope, with help from some of the crew members. Sadly, the noise they dismiss as coming from the ship's cat is actually the footsteps of Josephine's father, Captain Corcoran, who has been told of their plans to sneak away – and is armed with a very different kind of cat altogether.

ALL [much alarmed]:
 Goodness me—
 Why, what was that?

DICK:
 Silent be,
 It was the cat!

ALL [reassured]:
 It was – it was the cat!

CAPTAIN [producing cat-o'-nine-tails]:
 They're right – it was the cat!

28 March

'When a man loves cats, I am his friend and comrade, without further introduction.'

– Mark Twain

29 March

And I a smiling woman.
I am only thirty.
And like the cat I have nine times to die.

– Sylvia Plath, 'Lady Lazarus'

30 March

It is a very inconvenient habit of kittens (Alice had once made the remark) that, whatever you say to them, they always purr. 'If they would only purr for 'yes' and mew for 'no', or any rule of that sort,' she had said, 'so that one could keep up a conversation! But how can you talk with a person if they always say the same things?'

On this occasion, the kitten only purred; and it was impossible to guess whether it meant 'yes' or 'no'.

– Lewis Carroll, *Through the Looking-Glass, and What
Alice Found There*

31 MARCH

English poet and scholar John Donne died on this day in 1631. Biographer Katherine Rundell describes him delightfully: 'He wore a hat big enough to sail a cat in, a big lace collar, and exquisite moustache.' However, today's cat is found not in Donne's hat, but in his prose work *Devotions Upon Emergent Occasions*.

A man that is not afraid of a lion is afraid of a cat; not afraid of starving, and yet is afraid of some joint of meat at the table presented to feed him; not afraid of the sound of drums and trumpets and shot and those which they seek to drown, the last cries of men, and is afraid of some particular harmonious instrument; so much afraid as that with any of these the enemy might drive this man, otherwise valiant enough, out of the field.

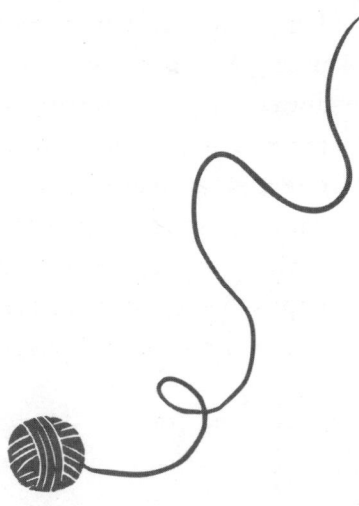

APRIL

S pring is officially here – though if you're in the UK, it's possible that nobody's told the weather that (see 15 April for a truly delightful description of a spring morning). April is a time when the world begins to wake up after lying dormant all winter, and you might start to feel more creative and inspired – so it seems fitting that we have plenty of poetry this month. All of it cat-based, of course.

This month we'll meet a not-very-wise but still altogether charming Angora cat (see 2 April), a human-sized tortoiseshell who works as a waiter (see 19 April) and not one but two of Terry Pratchett's feline creations, namely You and Greebo (see 13 and 28 April respectively).

Moveable feasts

EASTER: The Christian festival of Easter typically falls between 22 March and 25 April. (Technically, it is marked on the first Sunday after the full moon that occurs on or after the spring equinox, but in the interests of cat-like brevity, let's just say it usually happens in late March or April.) Unfortunately, cats are more likely to hunt the Easter Bunny than celebrate his coming (see 10 May for a cat-versus-rabbit showdown).

⁙

1 April

American essayist Agnes Repplier was born on this day in 1855. Her works covered literary criticism and observations on everyday life, but she also penned *The Fireside Sphinx* (1901), a beautifully written and whimsical cultural history of all things feline. We'll hear more from her next month, but for now, to mark her birthday, here is a passage from this collection of musings:

There are many who strange though it may appear prefer their chimney corner empty of delight. We hear these persons constantly complain [...] that if a cat be in the room with them, she singles them out to be the recipients of her attentions, rubbing herself against their feet, and showing an obstinate preference for their society.

[...] This is one of the traits of the impenetrable cat nature to which we hold no key. The dog is guided by a kindly instinct to the man or woman whose heart is open to his advances. The cat often leaves the friend who courts her, to honour, or to harass, the unfortunate mortal who shudders at her unwelcome caresses. There is an impish perversity about the deed which recalls the snares of witch craft. So, too, does her uncanny habit of looking with fixed gaze over one's shoulder at a dark corner of the room, and turning her head slightly from time to time, as her eyes follow the movements of the unseen object in the shadows. When I am alone of a winter's night, and oppressed by the vague fear of life and death which haunt the soul in moments of subjection, I find this steadfast stare at a ghostly presence trying to the nerves. The brilliancy of the cat's eyes, the narrowing of the lids, the stern contraction of the brow, the deadly repose of the whole figure, enhance the shadowy spell by which she dominates that hour.

2 APRIL

Today's cat is the narrator of Émile Zola's short story 'The Paradise of Cats', apparently related to the author by an Angora cat, 'the most stupid animal I know of'. The cat explains to him that one day, bored with his privileged existence, he escaped through a window and explored the lives of the street cats.

Three cats came rolling over from the top of a house towards me, mewing most frightfully, and as I was on the point of fainting away, they called me a silly thing, and said they were mewing for fun. I began mewing with them. It was charming.

3 APRIL

'Cats are the natural companions of intellectuals. They are silent watchers of dreams, inspiration and patient research.'

– Dr Fernand Méry

4 APRIL

Finnish poet Edith Södergran was born on this day in 1892. To mark the occasion, here are a few lines from her poem 'A Wish'.

In our entire sunny world,
I want but one thing: a garden bench
where a cat lies in the sun…

5 APRIL

Poet, playwright and novelist Algernon Charles Swinburne was born on this day in 1837. Among his many works is his feline-themed poem 'To a Cat', which opens:

Stately, kindly lordly friend,
Condescend
Here to sit by me , and turn
Glorious eyes that smile and burn,
Golden eyes, love's lustrous meed,
On the golden page I read.

We all know all too well that feeling of pleading with a cat to bestow its attention on you, and it is brilliantly captured here.

6 APRIL

On this day in 2010, the novel *Will Grayson, Will Grayson* by John Green and David Levithan was published. The book is best known for the unusual way it was written, with the co-authors each writing every other chapter, but it also has a running theme about cats – *Maybe Dead Cats*, to be precise. This is the name of a fictional band in the novel, who are themselves named in honour of Schrödinger's cat (see 12 August).

7 APRIL

Poet William Wordsworth was born on this day in 1770. To celebrate, today's cat is from his poem 'The Kitten and Falling Leaves'.

But the Kitten, how she starts,
Crouches, stretches, paws and darts!
First at one and then its fellow
Just as light and just as yellow.

8 April

Ernest Hemingway's love of cats is no secret, and indeed we'll return to this on 21 July and 25 November. Today, though, our focus is his short story 'The Cat in the Rain', in which a young American couple are staying in an Italian hotel. The wife notices a cat sheltering from the rain outside and tries to go and find it without success. Returning to the room, she laments her catlessness.

'Anyway, I want a cat,' she said. 'I want a cat. I want a cat now. If I can't have long hair or any fun, I can have a cat.'

9 April

French poet Charles Baudelaire was born on this day in 1821. Please enjoy these verses from his poem 'Cat'.

As if he owned the place, a cat
meanders through my mind,
sleek and proud, yet so discreet
in making known his will

that I hear music when he mews,
and even when he purrs
a tender timbre in the sound
compels my consciousness.

10 April

Today's cat is of the larger variety, as we share these lines from D H Lawrence's poem lamenting the death of a hunted mountain lion.

> And I think in this empty world there was room for me and a mountain lion.
> And I think in the world beyond, how easily we might spare a million or two humans
> And never miss them.
> Yet what a gap in the world, the missing white frost-face Of that slim yellow mountain lion!

> – 'Mountain Lion'

11 April

On this day in 1914, George Bernard Shaw's play *Pygmalion* opened in London after first being performed in Vienna. Although no cats are featured in the play, Shaw did refer to them in his essay 'Is There Any Hope in Education?'.

It is said that if you wash a cat it will never again wash itself. This may or may not be true: what is certain is that if you teach a man anything he will never learn it; and if you cure him of a disease he will be unable to cure himself the next time it attacks him. Therefore, if you want to see a cat clean, you throw a bucket of mud over it, [and] it will immediately take extraordinary pains to lick the mud off, and finally be cleaner than it was before.

12 April

Today marks the birthday of children's writer Beverly Cleary. Her novel *Socks* was originally published in 1974, and tells the story of Socks, a tabby cat with four white paws, who finds himself somewhat sidelined when his owners have a new baby.

> Then a strange thing happened. Mrs Bricker's lap began to shrink. One day Socks was perfectly comfortable resting on her knees, and the next day he didn't have enough room.

13 April

Today's cat is You, the white cat companion of Granny Weatherwax in Terry Pratchett's Discworld novels, who first appears as a kitten in *Wintersmith*. The name 'You' comes from 'You! Stop that!' and 'You! Get off there!'. Despite this, it's clear the little kitten is much loved by the gruff Granny Weatherwax.

> 'Granny, your hat squeaked,' said Tiffany. 'It went meep!'
> 'No it didn't,' Granny said sharply.
> 'It did, you know,' said Nanny Ogg. 'I heard it, too.'
> Granny Weatherwax grunted and pulled off her heat. The white kitten, curled around her tight bun of hair, blinked in the light.
> 'I can't help it,' Granny muttered. 'If I leave the dratted thing alone it goes under the dresser and cries and cries.' She looked around at the others as if daring them to say anything. 'Anyway,' she added, 'it keeps m'head warm.'

14 April

But cats to me are strange, so strange –
I cannot sleep if one is near

– W H Davies, 'The Cat'

15 April

Today's cat enjoys only the briefest of mentions in Virginia Woolf's experimental novel *The Waves* (see also 8 October), but this passage so beautifully captures the feel of a spring morning that it couldn't be missed.

In the garden the birds that had sung erratically and spasmodically in the dawn on that tree, on that bush, now sang together in chorus, shrill and sharp; now together, as if conscious of companionship, now alone as if to the pale blue sky. They swerved, all in one flight, when the black cat moved among the bushes, when the cook threw cinders on the ash heap and startled them. Fear was in their song, and apprehension of pain, and joy to be snatched quickly now at this instant. Also they sang emulously in the clear morning air, swerving high over the elm tree, singing together as they chased each other, escaping, pursuing, pecking each other as they turned high in the air. And then tiring of pursuit and flight, lovelily they came descending, delicately declining, dropped down and sat silent on the tree, on the wall, with their bright eyes glancing, and their heads turned this way, that way; aware, awake; intensely conscious of one thing, one object in particular.

16 APRIL

French poet and novelist Anatole France was born on this day in 1844. One of his first published prose works was the novella *The Famished Cat* – the title referring not to a hungry kitty, but to an establishment of the same name frequented by the novel's characters.

They stopped at the narrowest, the greasiest, the blackest, the smokiest, and the nastiest part of the Rue Saint-Jacques, and went into a shop full of little tables, at the end of which was a glass partition hung with white curtains. There were paintings on the walls, on the partition, on the ceiling even. […] Saint-Lucie, who was very fond of pictures, at once singled out the most arresting canvases – a raven in the snow, and the nude body of an old woman hanging head down; a raw sirloin of beef wrapped in a piece of paper; and above all, a gutter-cat on a roof among the chimney pots, outlining against an enormous ruddy moon its lean black back arched like a medieval bridge. This work, by a young master of the impressionist school, served as a sign for the establishment.

17 APRIL

Writer Nick Hornby was born on this day in 1957. To celebrate his birthday, today's literary cats are the figurative kittens mentioned in his bestselling 1995 novel *High Fidelity*.

I tried not to run Phil down too much – I felt bad enough as it was, what with screwing his girlfriend and all. But it became unavoidable, because when Jackie expressed doubts about him, I had to nurture those doubts as if they were tiny, sickly kittens, until eventually they became sturdy, healthy grievances, with their own cat doors, which allowed them to wander in and out of our conversation at will.

18 April

Anyone who has tried to write while owning a cat will agree that they have a particular skill for walking across your desk while you are mid-sentence. These days, it's more likely they'll delicately pick their way across your keyboard, but it seems the problem has been with us for centuries. In 2013, a doctoral student at the University of Sarajevo was searching through some medieval manuscripts from Dubrovnik, Croatia, when she noticed a set of centuries-old inky paw prints scattered across the page. In an interview, the student explained:

[You can imagine an] incident when a cat, presumably owned by the scribe, pounced first on the ink container and then on the book, branding it for the ensuing centuries. You can almost picture the writer shooing the cat in a panicky fashion while trying to remove it from his desk. Despite his best efforts the damage was already complete and there was nothing else he could have done but turn a new leaf and continue his job.

– Emir Filipović

19 April

In Mai Mochizuki's delightfully whimsical novel *The Full Moon Coffee Shop*, a series of Kyoto inhabitants each dealing with their own personal struggles stumble across a mysterious coffee shop. There is no menu – instead, the waiting staff will serve you what they think you most need. It's also worth mentioning that the waiting staff are enormous cats who can read horoscopes.

I turned around – and now found myself facing a huge tortoiseshell cat. It was proffering a tray in my direction… The creature must have been two metres tall. It was standing on its hind legs and wearing a navy-blue apron. Its face was perfectly round, its smiling eyes like crescent moons.

The cat was talking.

The cat was holding a tray.

Most of all, the cat was…enormous.

20 April

But what I do say is: that for straightfor'ard, level-headed reasoning, give me cats. [...] [A] cat, she's got her own opinion about human beings. She don't say much, but you can tell enough to make you anxious not to hear the whole of it. The consequence is, we says a cat's got no intelligence. That's where we let our prejudice steer our judgment wrong. In a matter of plain common sense, there ain't a cat living as couldn't take the lee side of a dog and fly round him. Now, have you ever noticed a dog at the end of a chain, trying to kill a cat as is sitting washing her face three-quarters of an inch out of his reach? Of course you have. Well, who's got the sense out of those two? The cat knows that it ain't in the nature of steel chains to stretch. The dog, who ought, you'd think, to know a durned sight more about 'em than she does, is sure they will if you only bark loud enough.

– Jerome K Jerome, *Novel Notes*

21 April

Charlotte Brontë was born on this day in 1816. To mark her birthday, here is a feline-themed extract from her novel *Vilette*, in which various characters creep about the garden by night on mysterious errands.

I looked. Behold Madame, in shawl, wrapping-gown, and slippers, softly descending the steps, and stealing like a cat round the garden: in two minutes she would have been upon Dr. John. If she were like a cat, however, he, quite as much, resembled a leopard: nothing could be lighter than his tread when he chose. He watched, and as she turned a corner, he took the garden at two noiseless bounds.

22 April

The way Dinah washed her kittens faces was this: first she held the poor thing down by its ear with one paw, and then with the other paw she rubbed its face all over, the wrong way, beginning at the nose: and just now, as I said, she was hard at work on the white kitten, which was lying quite still and trying to purr – no doubt feeling that it was all meant for its good.

– Lewis Carroll, *Through the Looking-Glass, and What
Alice Found There*

23 April

Playwright William Shakespeare is thought to have been born on this day in 1564 (and, indeed, to have died on the same date in 1616).

Tut, never fear me: I am as vigilant as a cat to steal cream.
– Falstaff, *Henry IV*, Part 1, Act IV, Scene 2

24 April

English novelist Daniel Defoe died on this day in 1731. In his famous work *Robinson Crusoe*, the title character finds himself stranded on an island after a shipwreck. For company, he has a parrot, along with a dog and the descendants of the two ship's cats, which he rescued from the wreckage.

It would have made a Stoic smile to have seen me and my little family sit down to dinner. [...] My dog, who was now grown old and crazy, and had found no species to multiply his kind upon, sat always at my right hand; and two cats, one on one side of the table and one on the other, expecting now and then a bit from my hand, as a mark of especial favour.

But these were not the two cats which I brought on shore at first, for they were both of them dead [...]; but one of them having multiplied by I know not what kind of creature, these were two which I had preserved tame; whereas the rest ran wild in the woods.

25 April

English poet William Cowper died on this day in 1800. In his honour, today's cat is his beloved pet and companion, and star of the poem 'The Retired Cat', which describes her fondness for finding cosy spots to snuggle up in – and an unfortunate incident which sees her trapped in a drawer after she climbs in for a snooze and an unsuspecting maid closes it.

A poet's cat, sedate and grave,
As poet well could wish to have,
Was much addicted to inquire
For nooks, to which she might retire,
And where, secure as mouse in chink,
She might repose, or sit and think.
I know not where she caught the trick—
Nature perhaps herself had cast her
In such a mould philosophique,
Or else she learn'd it of her master.
Sometimes ascending, debonnair,
An apple-tree or lofty pear,
Lodg'd with convenience in the fork,
She watch'd the gardener at his work;
Sometimes her ease and solace sought
In an old empty wat'ring-pot;
There, wanting nothing save a fan
To seem some nymph in her sedan,
Apparell'd in exactest sort,
And ready to be borne to court.

26 April

A cat's rage is beautiful, burning with a pure cat flame, all its hair standing up and crackling blue sparks, eyes blazing and sputtering.

– William S Burroughs, *The Cat Inside*

27 April

'Cat: a pygmy lion who loves mice, hates dogs and patronises human beings.'

– Oliver Herford

28 April

English author Terry Pratchett, best known for his beloved Discworld series, was born on this day in 1948. In his honour, today's cat is Greebo, a grumpy one-eyed cat belonging to Nanny Ogg. Greebo features in several Discworld novels, but one of his finest moments comes in *Witches Abroad*, when he catches and devours a bat, noting that it seems to be 'trying to change its shape, and he wasn't having any of that from a mouse with wings on'. The next day, the local villagers are seen rejoicing at the death of a vampire that had been terrorizing them.

Under the table, Greebo sat and washed himself. Occasionally he burped.

Vampires have risen from the dead, the grave and the crypt, but have never managed it from the cat.

29 April

On this day in 1963, Charles Bukowski wrote a letter to poet Neeli Cherry in which he observed:

> More and more black cats everywhere, but there's a white cat here, that means luck, brother. He has an angular scar down the left side of his head.
> Proud; a real shit-head.

30 April

Swedish writer and illustrator of children's books Sven Nordqvist was born on this day in 1946. It seems fitting, then, that today's cat is Findus, from his beloved series Pettson and Findus, about a farmer and his cat. Not only can Findus talk and walk on his hindlegs, but he's also a rather natty dresser, sporting a pair of green striped trousers.

MAY

Summer is almost here, gardens are blooming and, if you're lucky enough to have a cat, chances are they are spending their days lying in patches of sunshine and stalking through the newly lush grass. Our cats this month are a mixed bag: one is pink (see 6 May), one is an enormous vodka-sipping black tom (see 15 May), and one is worshipped as a god by rats in a sewer (see 8 May).

May is also Mental Health Month, so perhaps you'll be inspired to pay attention to your own wellbeing. Of course, nobody does this better than a cat, so make like a feline: protect your peace, seek out comfort at all costs and practise gratitude by purring to show that you're content (unless you are Purrless – see 8 March).

Moveable feasts

MOTHER'S DAY (US): See 'Moveable feasts' in March.

1 May

On this day in 1849, the first part of Dickens's *David Copperfield* was published in serial form (at the time, its title was the slightly wordier *The Personal History, Adventures, Experience, and Observation of David Copperfield the Younger, of Blunderstone Rookery*). As well as introducing readers to one of Dickens's best-loved protagonists, the story also includes many moments of the author's trademark wry humour, including Mr Dick's reaction to his less-than-roomy lodgings.

Mrs Crupp had indignantly assured him that there wasn't room to swing a cat there; but as Mr Dick justly observed to me, sitting down on the foot of the bed, nursing his leg, 'You know, Trotwood, I don't want to swing a cat. I never do swing a cat. Therefore, what does that signify to me!'

2 May

Superfans of Ann M Martin's The Babysitters Club series may know that today is the birthday of Mallory Pike, (fictional) member of said club and protagonist of the third book in the series, *Mallory and the Ghost Cat*. And the ghost cat isn't the only feline to feature in the series – the leader of The Babysitter's Club, Kristin or Kristy, owns a cat named Boo-Boo, and later one called Pumpkin.

3 MAY

If cats looked like frogs we'd realise what nasty, cruel little bastards they are. Style. That's what people remember.

– Terry Pratchett, *Lords and Ladies*

4 MAY

On 3 February, we learned about the *Ancrene Wisse* and its rules about cats. This text makes an appearance in *For thy Great Pain Have Mercy on My Little Pain* by Victoria Mackenzie, a beautiful reimagining of the lives of Julian of Norwich and Margery Kempe.

The *Ancrene Wisse* states that anchoresses may keep no animal but a cat. I have had several cats over the years, and they come and go from my cell as they please, without fear of excommunication. Indeed, my present cat fears nothing. I often joke with him, ask if he has been visiting witches. We keep this joke to ourselves, lest we're overheard and both of us drowned or burnt.

5 MAY

Some men there are love not a gaping pig;
Some, that are mad if they behold a cat.

– William Shakespeare, *The Merchant of Venice*,

Act IV, Scene 1

We'll have to agree to disagree on that one, Will – beholding a cat is surely a cause for delight, not fury.

6 MAY

Author and creator of *The Wonderful Wizard of Oz* L Frank Baum died on this day in 1919. Unless we're counting the Cowardly Lion, there aren't any cats in his most famous work, but later in the series, in the fourth book (*Dorothy and the Wizard in Oz*) we meet Eureka, who is today's cat.

At once a pink kitten crept out of the upset cage, sat down upon the glass roof, and yawned and blinked its round eyes.

'Oh,' said Dorothy. 'There's Eureka.'

'First time I ever saw a pink cat,' said Zeb.

'Eureka isn't pink; she's white. It's this queer light that gives her that colour.'

'Where's my milk?' asked the kitten, looking up into Dorothy's face. 'I'm almost starved to death.'

'Oh, Eureka! Can you talk?'

'Talk! Am I talking? Good gracious, I believe I am. Isn't it funny?' asked the kitten.

7 MAY

Legendary author Angela Carter was born on this day in 1940, and so today's cat is Figaro, the star of the short story 'Puss in Boots' from her seminal collection of darkly retold fairy tales, *The Bloody Chamber.*

[T]his little Figaro can slip into my lady's chamber smart as you like at any time whatsoever that he takes the fancy for, don't you know, he's a cat of the world, cosmopolitan, sophisticated; he can tell when a furry friend is the Missus' best company. For what lady in all the world could say 'no' to the passionate yet toujours discret advances of a fine marmalade cat?

8 MAY

Children's and YA novelist Robin Jarvis was born on this day in 1963. In his honour, today's cat comes from his series The Deptford Mice: Jupiter, 'the great dark God of the Sewers' – although it should be noted that none of his worshippers (a league of rats) know he's a cat.

Jupiter's iron claws dug into the bricks as he hauled himself forward.

'Yes,' he gloated. 'All these years, all this time I have laid hidden and secret from my subjects. Think of it – a cat worshipped as a god by rats!'

– *The Dark Portal*

9 May

The cat is sometimes inaccurately described as a domesticated animal. Fundamentally, he is no more domesticated than a crocodile. Certainly, he likes warmth, comfort and good food, and since he can most easily be provided with these good things by attaching himself to a human household he usually chooses to do [just that].

— Michael Joseph, *Cat's Company*

10 May

Novelist Richard Adams was born on this day in 1920. He is best known for his novel *Watership Down*, a tale of a group of rabbits who are forced to seek out a new home when their warrens are destroyed. As with *Mrs Frisby and the Rats of NIMH* (see 11 January) and The Deptford Mice (see 8 May), when the heroes are small prey animals, the villains are, all too often, feline. In this extract, brave bunnies Hazel and Pipkin find themselves faced with a cat.

The cat flung itself across the yard and the two rabbits leaped into flight with great thrusts of their hind legs. The cat came very fast indeed and although both of them had been braced ready to move on the instant, they were barely out of the yard in time. [...] From the cover of the hedge beside the lane they turned and looked back. The cat had stopped short and was licking one paw with a pretence of nonchalance.

'They hate to look silly,' said Hazel.

11 MAY

Author Sheila Burnford was born on this day in 1918. She is best known for her novel *The Incredible Journey*, which tells the tale of two dogs and a cat becoming separated from their family and making their way home through the wilderness. And so, today's feline is Tao, the Siamese cat who helps his canine friends survive by hunting for food as they make their way 300 miles across Canada.

12 MAY

Beloved poet and purveyor of nonsense Edward Lear was born on this day in 1812. And what book on literary cats could be complete without 'The Owl and the Pussy-Cat'?

The Owl and the Pussy-Cat went to sea
In a beautiful pea-green boat:
They took some honey, and plenty of money
Wrapped up in a five-pound note.
The Owl looked up to the stars above,
And sang to a small guitar,
'O lovely Pussy, O Pussy, my love,
What a beautiful Pussy you are,
You are,
You are!
What a beautiful Pussy you are!

Pussy said to the Owl, 'You elegant fowl,
How charmingly sweet you sing!
Oh! let us be married; too long we have tarried:
But what shall we do for a ring?'
They sailed away, for a year and a day,
To the land where the bong-tree grows;
And there in a wood a Piggy-wig stood,
With a ring at the end of his nose,
His nose,
His nose,
With a ring at the end of his nose.

'Dear Pig, are you willing to sell for one shilling
Your ring?' Said the Piggy, 'I will.'
So they took it away, and were married next day
By the Turkey who lives on the hill.
They dined on mince and slices of quince,
Which they ate with a runcible spoon;
And hand in hand, on the edge of the sand,
They danced by the light of the moon,
The moon,
The moon,
They danced by the light of the moon.

Lear had a much-loved cat pet cat called Foss, about whom
we'll learn more on 26 November.

13 MAY

Today's cat is Graymalk, the feline familiar of the witch Crazy Jill from the novel *A Night in the Lonesome October* by Roger Zelazny (born on this day in 1937). Although the novel's central character and narrator is Snuff, the dog familiar of Jack the Ripper, Graymalk has several pleasing scene-stealing moments, including during the exchange below, which comes after she has shared useful information with Snuff.

'Why do you tell me this?'

'Perhaps because I am a cat and it amuses me to be arbitrary and do you a good turn.'

14 MAY

I came to live in cat country. The houses are old and they have narrow gardens with walls. [...] Cats thrive here. There are always cats on the walls, roofs, and in the gardens, living a complicated secret life, like the neighbourhood lives of children that go on according to unimagined private rules the grown-ups never guess at.

– Doris Lessing, *Particularly Cats*

15 MAY

Russian writer Mikhail Bulgakov was born on this day in 1891. He is perhaps most famous for his surreal and mind-bending novel *The Master and Margarita*, and so in his honour today's cat is Behemoth, an enormous chess-playing feline with a penchant for pickled mushrooms and swinging from chandeliers (see 11 December).

> But there proved to be even worse things in the bedroom: on the jeweller's wife's pouffe there lounged in a free-and-easy pose a third figure – namely, a black cat of awesome dimensions with a shot glass of vodka in one paw and a fork, on which he had managed to spear a pickled mushroom, in the other.

16 MAY

Cats often appear in the work of Joyce Carol Oates (see also 3 March). Today's cat is Miranda, the exquisitely beautiful white Persian cat at the centre of her short story 'The White Cat' (itself inspired by Edgar Allan Poe's 'The Black Cat' – see 19 August).

> But of course, as Alissa acknowledged, a cat can't be forced to do anything against her will. 'It seems almost to be a law of nature,' she said solemnly.

17 MAY

[T]here is nothing so lowering to one's self-esteem as the affectionate contempt of a cat.

– Agnes Repplier, *The Fireside Sphinx*

18 MAY

Cats seem to go on the principle that it never does any harm to ask for what you want.

– Joseph Wood Krutch, *The Twelve Seasons*

19 MAY

American author Jodi Picoult was born on this day in 1966. To mark the occasion, please enjoy this short extract from one of her most famous novels, *My Sister's Keeper*.

That's the life, she said to me, as we watched a puppy chase its own tail. That's what I want to be next.

I had laughed. You would wind up as a cat, I told her. They don't need anyone else.

I need you, she replied.

Well, I said. Maybe I'll come back as catnip.

20 MAY

English poet Christopher Smart died on this day in 1771. In his honour, today's cat is Jeoffry, his beloved companion and inspiration for the poem 'Jubilate Agno' quoted below.

For I will consider my Cat Jeoffry.
For he is the servant of the Living God duly and daily serving him.
For at the first glance of the glory of God in the East he worships in his way.
For this is done by wreathing his body seven times round with elegant quickness.
For then he leaps up to catch the musk, which is the blessing of God upon his prayer.
For he rolls upon prank to work it in.
For having done duty and received blessing he begins to consider himself.
For this he performs in ten degrees.
For first he looks upon his forepaws to see if they are clean.
For secondly he kicks up behind to clear away there.
For thirdly he works it upon stretch with the forepaws extended.
For fourthly he sharpens his paws by wood.
For fifthly he washes himself.
For sixthly he rolls upon wash.
For seventhly he fleas himself, that he may not be interrupted upon the beat.
For eighthly he rubs himself against a post.
For ninthly he looks up for his instructions.
For tenthly he goes in quest of food.

21 MAY

Following on from yesterday's entry, we're spending our day with Jeoffry again – this time in the work of author Oliver Soden, who was inspired by Smart's poem to create a semifictionalized autobiography for this very special cat. In the passage below, Jeoffry meets someone rather regal.

[...] Jeoffry was just about to return home, when a carriage drew up that he knew, somehow, as cats can know things they should not, was different from the other vehicles that thundered their way in and out of his life. Crowds were gathered, shouting, cheering. [...] A trumpeter heralded the opening of the door [...], which opened (Jeoffry prowled closer) to reveal a grand boot, a buckle of astonishing glitter, a white stockinged leg into which a garter of gold thread appeared to slice painfully. [...] The face, all but hidden by the brocaded stomach beneath it, peered mistily down, and looked at Jeoffry. Jeoffry looked up into the face. The face went on its way, but had smiled, briefly. For a cat may look at a king.

– Jeoffrey: The Poet's Cat

22 MAY

Cats, though small in stature, have their own worlds.
From the moment they step into a new world, they're
already looking towards the future.

– Syou Ishida, *We'll Prescribe You a Cat*

23 MAY

English poet Thomas Hood was born on this day in 1799.
Let's celebrate with his poem 'Choosing their names', about
selecting monikers for cats.

Our old cat has kittens three
And I fancy these their names will be:
Pepperpot, Sootikin, Scratchaway-There!
Were ever kittens with these to compare?
And we call the old mother –
Now, what do you think?
Tabitha Longclaws Tiddley Wink.

24 MAY

Today's cat is Aristotle, the star of Dick King-Smith's children's book of the same name. Aristotle is a little white cat who lives with a wise, kind witch named Bella Donna. He's a little accident-prone – so it's lucky cats have nine lives.

25 MAY

Fans of Douglas Adams's The Hitchhiker's Guide to the Galaxy series may already be aware that 25 May is Towel Day, the day on which fans of the books carry a towel with them to show their love for the book (in which a towel is described as 'about the most massively useful thing an interstellar hitchhiker can have'). To mark the occasion, today's cat is The Lord, the pet of the ruler of the Universe – and one of the few things the ruler believes in.

> 'It's nothing to do with me,' [the ruler] said, 'I am not involved with people. The Lord knows I am not a cruel man.'
>
> 'Ah!' barked Zarniwoop, 'you say, 'The Lord'. You believe in something!'
>
> 'My cat,' said the man benignly, picking it up and stroking it. 'I call him The Lord. I am kind to him.'
>
> *– The Restaurant at the End of the Universe*

26 May

Alas! women are susceptible to practicalities no less than to good looks; cats chase mice as well as birds.

– Victor Hugo, *Les Misérables*

27 May

Cats were the gangsters of the animal world, living outside the law and often dying there. There were a great many of them who never grew old by the fire.

– Stephen King, *Pet Sematary*

28 May

French author Muriel Barbery was born on this day in 1969. Her bestselling 2006 novel *The Elegance of the Hedgehog* features a cat named Leo, after Leo Tolstoy, the pet cat and companion of the novel's main character Renée, a building concierge who chooses to conceal her refined tastes in art, literature and music. However, today's cat is another feline from the novel: Constitution, the pet of the book's other key character, Paloma.

At the moment, as I am writing, Constitution the cat is going by with her tummy dragging close to the floor. This cat has absolutely nothing constructive to do in life and still she is heading toward something, probably an armchair.

29 MAY

The first part of Haruki Murakami's novel *IQ84* was published in Japan on this day in 2009 (with the rest following in April 2010). Among its complex, interweaving plot, Murakami has one of the main characters, Tengo, read a short story called 'Town of Cats'.

> When the sun starts to go down, many cats cross the bridge into town – cats of all different kinds and colours. They are much larger than ordinary cats, but they are still cats. [...] The cats go about their business raising the shop shutters or seating themselves at their town hall desks to start their day's work.

30 MAY

The much-loved YA novel *The Princess Diaries* by Meg Cabot was first published on this day in 2000. To mark the occasion, today's cat is Fat Louie, feline companion of the soon-to-be princess, Mia.

I CAN'T move to Genovia, I just CAN'T!! Who would look after Fat Louie? My mom can't. She forgets to feed herself, let alone a CAT. I'm sure they won't let me have a cat in the palace. At least, not a cat like Louie, who weights twenty-five pounds and eats socks.

31 MAY

If you are reading a large newspaper, all spread out on the table, your cat will come and sit on the very paragraph you are reading, the talented cat draping her tail with miraculous precision over the very line you're not finished with.

– Leonore Fleischer, *The Cat's Pajamas*

JUNE

We're halfway through the year, and summer is finally with us. Perhaps you'll spend your month sipping tea in a vicarage garden with Agatha Christie (see 1 and 5 June), or attempting to make your way through the eight hundred-plus pages of *Ulysses* (see 16 June). Whatever you do, do it with a cat in your lap and a book in your hand.

This month we'll meet a sphinx (see 11 June), a rather greedy tiger (see 14 June) and a deceased feline whose owner hopes to turn it into a mummy (see 28 June).

Moveable feasts

FATHER'S DAY: Father's Day is usually celebrated on the third Sunday in June. Although cats are often more associated with women, let's take a moment to cherish all the cat dads out there. Two favourites have to be Samuel Johnson, who adored his cat Hodge (see 18 September), and Edward Lear, who was devoted to his feline companion Foss (see 26 November).

1 JUNE

June 1950 saw the publication of a classic Agatha Christie whodunnit, *A Murder is Announced*. As with all of Christie's best work, the book features a cast of intriguing and often amusing characters – and also a cat with a rather unusual name.

> And Butt was saying only the other day [...] that we've got real culture here in Chipping Cleghorn. [...] Our Vicar's a highly educated gentleman. [...] And even the vicarage cat, Butt says, is called after an Assyrian king! [...] Come along, Tiglath Pileser, you shall have the herring bones.

2 June

Novelist and poet Thomas Hardy was born on this day in 1840. Best known for works including *Far from the Madding Crowd* and *Tess of the d'Urbervilles*, he also penned a rather touching poem on the death of a beloved pet: 'Last Words to a Dumb Friend'.

Pet was never mourned as you,
Purrer of the spotless hue,
Plumy tail, and wistful gaze
While you humoured our queer ways,
Or outshrilled your morning call
Up the stairs and through the hall -
Foot suspended in its fall -
While, expectant, you would stand
Arched, to meet the stroking hand;
Till your way you chose to wend
Yonder, to your tragic end.

3 June

American poet and writer Allen Ginsberg was born on this day in 1926. As a member of the Beat generation, Ginsberg was probably more likely to use the word 'cat' to refer to a person than a pet, but on 9 November 1954, he did write in a letter to Jack Kerouac: 'A cat by the way sits on my shoulder as I write this.' Presumably this cat was of the feline variety.

4 June

Cats always pick the laps of people who don't like them.

– Barbara Michaels, *Vanish with the Rose*

5 June

After the rather impressively named Tiglath Pileser of 1 June, today's cat is another of Agatha Christie's felines, but this time with a slightly less grandiose moniker: Wonky Pooh the cat, from her 1939 novel *Murder is Easy*. And this orange Persian cat isn't just there to provide a little light relief – he may even have played a role in one of the novel's many murders.

Miss Waynflete addressed him in a cooing voice.

'Why, Wonky Pooh! Where's my Wonky Pooh been all the morning?'

6 June

We'll hear more about H P Lovecraft, author of the chilling, unnerving and downright weird, on 20 August, but for now, here's a brief extract from one of his essays.

It is good to be a cynic – it is better to be a contented cat – and it is best not to exist at all.

– 'Nietzscheism and Realism'

7 June

It always gives me a shiver when I see a cat seeing what I can't see.

— Eleanor Farjeon, *Faithful Jenny Dove and Other Tales*

8 June

Cats have no sense of humour, they have terribly inflated egos, and they are very touchy. If somebody asked me why it was worth anyone's time to cater to them I would be forced to answer that there is no logical reason.

— Robert A Heinlein, *The Door into Summer*

9 June

Japanese author Hiro Arikawa was born on this day in 1972, so today's cat is Nana, the protagonist of her bestselling novel *The Travelling Cat Chronicles*.

At that moment, we were without doubt the greatest travellers in the world. And I was the world's greatest travelling cat.

Rachel Yoder's ferocious debut novel, *Nightbitch*, tells the story of a young mother who suspects she may be turning into a dog. The story is steeped in magical realism and an underlying thread of darkness. It also features a very beautiful black cat – although it's fair to say that cat-lovers should proceed with caution.

> [The cat] was astoundingly beautiful and, to the same degree, astoundingly idiotic. She meowed frantically until someone walked over to the bowl and pointed at her food and shook it around a bit, at which point she began to eat as if starved. She always darted in the same direction the mother was walking, and then got stepped on, then made a horrid noise and rocketed off to the basement.

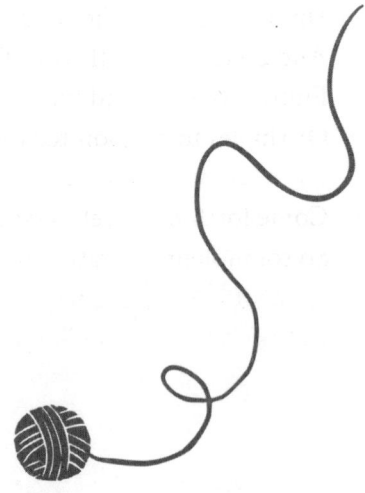

11 June

On this day in 1894, Oscar Wilde's lengthy poem 'The Sphinx' was published. In it, the poem's narrator questions a sphinx (a mythical creature usually depicted as having the head of a human, the body of a lion and the wings of an eagle) about her life – and, particularly, her loves, seeming torn between admiration and distaste.

In a dim corner of my room
For longer than my fancy thinks,
A beautiful and silent Sphinx
Has watched me through the shifting gloom.

Inviolate and immobile
She does not rise she does not stir
For silver moons are nought to her
And nought to her the suns that reel.
[...]
Upon the mat she lies and leers
And on the tawny throat of her
Flutters the soft and fur
Or ripples to her pointed ears.

Come forth my lovely seneschal!
So somnolent, so statuesque!
Come forth you exquisite grotesque!
Half woman and half animal!

12 June

Author Paul Gallico might be best known for his 1941 novella *The Snow Goose*, but much of his literary output was cat-focused, including *Honorable Cat* (see 10 February) and *The Silent Miaow: A Manual for Kittens, Strays, and Homeless Cats*, which contains advice to help felines find (and ultimately be served by) a human family. But today's cat is Thomasina, star of *Thomasina, the Cat Who Thought She Was God*. This ginger-furred feline who awakens after a cruel man has attempted to kill her with no memory of her previous life and a conviction that she is the resurrection of the Egyptian cat goddess Bastet.

> God I have been – God I am. But quite frankly, sometimes it is all just a little too much for one small cat. The demands made upon me!

13 June

Poet William Butler Yeats was born on this day in 1865. Here's a verse from his poem about an unlikely pair: a cat and a hare.

A speckled cat and a tame hare
Eat at my hearthstone
And sleep there;
And both look up to me alone
For learning and defence
As I look up to Providence.

– 'Two Songs of a Fool'

14 June

Writer and illustrator Judith Kerr was born on this day in 1923. As well as creating the popular picture-book cat Mog (who we'll be seeing on 22 December), Kerr is also the brilliant mind behind *The Tiger Who Came to Tea*, an endlessly popular story about a tiger inviting himself into the home of little Sophie and her mother, before devouring all the food and drink in the house.

15 JUNE

Nothing looks as self-satisfied as a contented cat.
— Elizabeth Peters, *Seeing a Large Cat*

16 JUNE

Today is Bloomsday, the day immortalized in James Joyce's epic and meandering work *Ulysses*. On this day, it's traditional for lovers of the book to gather and read aloud from its pages. As all good books do, the novel features a cat – and also Joyce's remarkably accurate rendering of a miaow.

The cat walked stiffly round a leg of the table with tail on high.

– Mkgnao!

– O, there you are, Mr Bloom said, turning from the fire.

The cat mewed in answer and stalked again stiffly round a leg of the table, mewing. Just how she stalks over my writingtable. Prr. Scratch my head. Prr.

Mr Bloom watched curiously, kindly, the lithe black form. Clean to see: the gloss of her sleek hide, the white button under the butt of her tail, the green flashing eyes. He bent down to her, his hands on his knees.

– Milk for the pussens, he said.

– Mrkgnao! the cat cried.

They call them stupid. They understand what we say better than we understand them.

17 JUNE

There was a kind of balustrade which served as a backrest a little way out from the wall, and in the cagelike space, a cat was miaowing. How had it slipped in there? It was too big to get out. Evening was coming on; a woman came up to the bench, a paper bag in her hand, and produced some scraps of meat. These she fed to the cat, stroking it tenderly the while.

– Simone de Beauvoir, *The Prime of Life*

18 JUNE

In one chapter of Mark Twain's 1872 novel *Roughing It*, he shares the story of Dick Baker, 'one of the gentlest spirits that ever bore its patient cross in weary exile':

Whenever he was out of luck and a little down-hearted, [Dick] would fall to mourning over the loss of a wonderful cat he used to own (for where women and children are not, men of kindly impulses take up with pets, for they must love something). And he always spoke of the strange sagacity of that cat with the air of a man who believed in his secret heart that there was something human about it – maybe even supernatural.

19 June

In John Holman's creative and sometimes elusive novel *Luminous Mysteries*, one of the main characters, Grim, suffers a motorcycle accident. While he lies unconscious in a hospital bed, his mind creates an alternate reality in which he is a dog, conversing with another dog on whether dogs and cats can become romantically involved.

'Can't dogs love cats?'
'That's not the point. Some dogs, some cats, sure. You should see her writhing on concrete in the sun.'

20 June

American writer Lilian Jackson Braun was born on this day in 1913. She wrote the mystery series The Cat Who…, made up of twenty-nine novels featuring a reporter and his two Siamese cats, Koko and Yum Yum, who help him solve mysteries.

To understand a cat, you must realize that he has his own gifts, his own viewpoint, even his own morality.
– *The Cat Who Could Read Backwards*

21 June

The cat is, above all things, a dramatist; its life is lived in an endless romance though the drama is played out on quite another stage than our own, and we only enter into it as subordinate characters, as stage managers, or rather stage carpenters.

– Margaret Benson, *The Soul of a Cat and Other Stories*

22 June

English poet and writer Walter de la Mare died on this day in 1956. In his honour, here is 'Five Eyes', a poem about a miller named Hans and his three black cats:

In Hans' old Mill his three black cats
Watch the bins for the thieving rats.
Whisker and claw, they crouch in the night,
Their five eyes smouldering green and bright:
Squeaks from the flour sacks, squeaks from where
The cold wind stirs on the empty stair,
Squeaking and scampering, everywhere.
Then down they pounce, now in, now out,
At whisking tail, and sniffing snout;
While lean old Hans he snores away
Till peep of light at break of day;
Then up he climbs to his creaking mill,
Out come his cats all grey with meal -
Jekkel, and Jessup, and one-eyed Jill.

23 June

Following our introduction to Behemoth on 15 May, here is another golden moment with one of literature's most famous (and naughtiest) cats.

Standing on his hindlegs and covered in dust, the cat was meanwhile bowing in greeting before Margarita. Around the cat's neck there was now a white dress tie, done up in a bow, and on his chest a lady's mother-of-pearl opera glass on a strap. In addition to this, the cat's whiskers were gilt.

'Now, what's all this?' exclaimed Woland. 'Why have you gilded your whiskers? And why the devil do you need a tie if you've got no trousers on?'

'A cat isn't meant to wear trousers, Messire,' replied the cat with great dignity. 'Perhaps you'll require me to don boots as well. Only in fairy tales is there a puss in boots, Messire. But have you ever seen anyone at a ball without a tie? I don't intend to find myself in a comical situation and risk being thrown out on my ear! Everyone adorns himself in whatever way he can. Consider what has been said to apply to the opera glass too, Messire!'

– Mikhail Bulgakov, *The Master and Margarita*

24 June

On this day in 1848, Anne Brontë's novel *The Tenant of Wildfell Hall* was published. To mark the occasion, here is a feline-focused passage, which occurs when the narrator, Gilbert Markham, is sitting by the fire with Mary and Eliza Willward.

[...] We seemed, indeed, to be mutually pleased with each other, and managed to maintain between us a cheerful and animated, though not very profound conversation. It was little better than a tête-à-tête, for Miss Millward never opened her lips, except occasionally to correct some random assertion or exaggerate expression of her sister's, and once to ask her to pick up the ball of cotton, that had rolled under the table. I did this myself, however, as in duty bound.

'Thank you, Mr Markham,' said she, as I presented it to her. 'I would have picked it up myself; only I did not want to disturb the cat.'

'Mary, dear, that won't excuse you in Mr Markham's eyes,' said Eliza; 'he hates cats, I dare say, as cordially as he does old maids – like all other gentlemen – don't you, Mr Markham?'

'I believe it is natural for our unamiable sex, to dislike the creatures,' replied I; 'for you ladies lavish so many caresses upon them.'

'Bless them – little darlings!' cried she, in a sudden burst of enthusiasm, turning round and overwhelming her sister's pet with a shower of kisses.

25 June

George Orwell was born on this day in 1903. To mark his birthday, today's feline is, of course, the cat from his novel *Animal Farm*.

Last of all came the cat, who looked around, as usual, for the warmest place, and finally squeezed herself in between Boxer and Clover; there she purred contentedly throughout Major's speech without listening to a word of what he was saying.

26 June

The only things in the kitchen that did not sneeze, were the cook, and a large cat which was sitting on the hearth and grinning from ear to ear.

'Please would you tell me,' said Alice, a little timidly, for she was not quite sure whether it was good manners for her to speak first, 'why your cat grins like that?'

'It's a Cheshire cat,' said the Duchess. 'And that's why.'
[...]

'I didn't know that Cheshire cats always grinned; in fact, I didn't know that cats could grin.'

'They all can,' said the Duchess. 'And most of 'em do.'

–Lewis Carroll, *Alice's Adventures in Wonderland*

27 June

Cats have a way of always having been there even if they've only just arrived. They move in their own personal time. They act as if the human world is one they just happened to have stopped off in, on their way to somewhere that is probably a whole lot more interesting.

– Terry Pratchett, *The Unadulterated Cat*

28 June

Today's cat is Mabel from Jacqueline Wilson's *The Cat Mummy*. Sadly, poor Mabel is an older cat, and only makes it a few chapters into the book. Her owner, Verity, finds her body curled up in a wardrobe. And Verity has been learning about the ancient Egyptians at school...

Then it came to me. It was as if the great cat goddess Bastet had put her holy paw upon me to give the idea. I would make Mabel into a mummy!

29 JUNE

Today's cat is the aptly named Book, the bookshop cat from V E Schwab's novel *The Invisible Life of Addie La Rue*. He provides some welcome comfort in the pages of a book about making dark deals with sinister forces.

Henry scoops a handful of kibble into the small red dish behind the counter for Book, the shop's ancient cat, and a moment later, a ratty orange head pokes up over the chapbooks in POETRY. The cat likes to climb behind a stack and sleep for days, his presence marked only by the emptying dish and the occasional gasp of a customer when they come across a pair of unblinking yellow eyes at the back of the shelves.

30 JUNE

Margaret Mitchell's iconic novel *Gone with the Wind* was published on this day in 1936. Mitchell was a known cat-lover – one of the most famous images of her shows her as a young woman with cat in her arms – and so today's cat is Tom, who makes a brief appearance in the pages of her book.

> For comfort, he made overtures to the honey-coloured cat which lay on the sunny window sill in the front hall. But Tom, full of years and irritable at disturbances, switched his tail and spat softly.

JULY

July is all about blue skies, warm days and balmy evenings; essentially, it's the perfect month for cats, and you'll often find them snoozing away the afternoon in a shady spot in the garden, which seems like a very civilized way to pass the summer.

This month, we'll be spending some time with Henry David Thoreau in *Walden* (see 4 July) and paying a visit to the vast, crumbling castle of *Gormenghast* (see 9 July). Along the way, we'll meet a talking cat (see 3 July), a whiskered sous chef (see 31 July) and a feline who is truly electric (see 10 July). Most of all, though, we'll be hanging out with writers who adored cats, including Ernest Hemingway, Raymond Chandler and Emily Brontë.

1 July

[C]ats, I always think, only jump into your lap to check
if you are cold enough, yet, to eat.

– Anne Enright, *The Gathering*

2 July

A cat actually thinks visibly. If you watch him jump on
a shelf, the wish to jump and the action of jumping are
one and the same thing.

– John Heilpern, *Conference of the Birds: The Story of
Peter Brook in Africa*

3 JULY

Czech novelist Franz Kafka was born on this day in 1883. Although some cats do feature in his work – the paragraph-long short story 'A Little Fable' being a particular highlight – today we're turning to another book by the famed cat-lover Haruki Murakami – *Kafka on the Shore*.

The black cat slowly stretched out a leg, then narrowed its eyes and gave the old man another good long look.

With a big grin on his face, the man stared right back. The cat hesitated for a time, then plunged ahead and spoke. 'Hmm...so you're able to speak.'

'That's right,' the old man said bashfully. To show his respect, he took off his threadbare cotton hiking hat. 'Not that I can speak to every cat I meet, but if things go well I can. Like right now.'

4 JULY

On this day in 1845, American writer and naturalist Henry David Thoreau moved to Walden Pond, where he built a cabin and lived alone for two years, two months and two days. The experience informed much of his writing, most famously his celebrated book *Walden*. In the passage below, he muses on some encounters with cats – and a strange winged cat creature of which he's heard rumours.

Once I was surprised to see a cat walking along the stony shore of the pond, for they rarely wander so far from home. The surprise was mutual. Nevertheless the most domestic cat, which has lain on a rug all her days, appears quite at home in the woods, and, by her sly and stealthy behaviour, proves herself more native there than the regular inhabitants. Once, when berrying, I met with a cat with young kittens in the woods, quite wild, and they all, like their mother, had their backs up and were fiercely spitting at me. A few years before I lived in the woods there was what was called a 'winged cat' in one of the farm-houses in Lincoln nearest the pond, Mr. Gilian Baker's. When I called to see her in June, 1842, she was gone a-hunting in the woods, as was her wont, (I am not sure whether it was a male or female, and so use the more common pronoun,) but her mistress told me that she came into the neighbourhood a little more than a year before, in April, and was finally taken into their house; that she was of a dark brownish-gray colour, with a white spot on her throat, and white feet, and had a large bushy tail like a fox; that in the winter the fur grew thick and flatted out along her sides, forming stripes ten or twelve inches long by two and a half wide, and under her chin like a muff, the upper side loose, the under matted like felt, and in the spring these appendages dropped off. They gave me a pair of her 'wings,' which I keep still. There is no appearance of a membrane about them. Some thought it was part flying-squirrel or some other wild animal, which is not impossible, for, according to naturalists, prolific hybrids have been produced by the union of the marten and domestic cat. This would have been the right kind of cat for me to keep, if I had kept any; for why should not a poet's cat be winged as well as his horse?

5 July

Children's book author Jill Murphy was born on this day in 1949. She is perhaps best known for her much-loved The Worst Witch series, featuring the hapless Mildred Hubble as a witch in training. During their first term, all the other students at Miss Cackle's Academy for Witches are given black cats in true witchy style – but Mildred's companion is the rather less dramatic looking Tabby.

Mildred was the last of all, and then she reached the table Miss Cackle pulled out of the basket not a sleek black kitten like all the others but a little tabby with white paws and the sort of fur that looked as if it had been out all night in a gale.

6 July

Author Hilary Mantel was born on this day in 1952. To mark the date, today's cat is from her novel *Wolf Hall*: Marlinspike, the kitten born to a cat hiding in Cardinal Wolsey's rooms, and adopted by Thomas Cromwell.

[F]or a while, the cardinal is amused, and puts the kittens on a cushion in an open chest, and watches as they grow. One of them is black and hungry, with a coat like wool and yellow eyes. When it is weaned, he brings it home. He takes it from under his coat, where it has been sleeping curled against his shoulder. 'Gregory, look.' He holds it out to his son. 'I am a giant, my name is Marlinspike.'

7 July

Science-fiction writer and cat-lover Robert A Heinlein was born on this day in 1907. In his honour, today's cat is Pixel, the title character of Heinlein's 1985 novel *The Cat Who Walks Through Walls*. The ever-present Pixel has a knack for showing up wherever the book's narrator, Colonel Colin Campbell (who also goes by Richard), finds himself, and, as the title suggests, even manages to walk through a wall. Here's Campbell's first introduction to this fantastical feline.

> Galahad surrounded the kitten with his left hand. 'This is Pixel. Pixel, may I present Richard? Richard, we are honoured to have been joined by Lord Pixel, cadet feline in residence.
>
> 'How do you do, Pixel?'

8 July

Cats on pavements, cats on garden walls, or coming towards you from doorways, stretch and wave their tails, they greet you, walk a few steps with you. They want companionship or, if they are shut out by heartless owners […] they appeal for help with the loud insistent demanding miaow that means they are hungry or thirsty or cold. A cat winding around your legs at a street corner might be wondering if he can exchange a poor home for a better one.

– Doris Lessing, 'Rufus the Survivor'

9 July

Writer Mervyn Peake was born on this day in 1911. He's best known for his Gormenghast books, a fantastical and surreal series about the inhabitants of the sprawling Castle Gormenghast. And you'll be delighted to hear that some of those inhabitants are cats.

A room was filled with the late sunbeams. Steerpike stood quite still, a twinge of pleasure running through his body. He grinned. A carpet filled the floor with blue pasture. Thereon were seated in a hundred decorative attitudes, or stood immobile like carvings, or walked superbly across their sapphire setting, inter-weaving with each other like a living arabesque, a swarm of snow-white cats.

[...] As they passed through a carved archway at the end of the room and had closed the door behind them he heard the vibration of their throats, for now that the white cats were once more alone it was revived, and the deep unhurried purring was like the voice of an ocean in the throat of a shell.

10 July

Serbian-American engineer and inventor Nikola Tesla was born on this day in 1856. In his honour, today's cat is his 'magnificent Mačak – the finest of all cats in the world'. In a letter written in 1939, Tesla credited a childhood experience with Mačak sparking his interest in electricity.

In the dusk of the evening light, as I stroked Mačak's back, I saw a miracle that made me speechless with amazement. Mačak's back was a sheet of light and my hand produced a shower of sparks loud enough to be heard all over the house. My father was a very learned man; he had an answer for every question. But this phenomenon was new even to him. 'Well,' he finally remarked, 'this is nothing but electricity, the same thing you see through the trees in a storm.'

My mother seemed charmed. 'Stop playing with this cat,' she said. 'He might start a fire.' But I was thinking abstractedly. Is nature a gigantic cat? If so, who strokes its back?

11 July

The domestic cat is a contradiction. No animal has developed such an intimate relationship with mankind, while at the same time demanding and getting such independence of movement and action. The dog may be man's best friend, but it is rarely allowed out on its own to wander from garden to garden or street to street. The obedient dog has to be taken for a walk. The headstrong cat walks alone.

– Desmond Morris, *Catwatching*

12 July

Chilean poet Pablo Neruda was born on this day in 1904. He wrote several poems about our feline friends (see also 20 December). Today, enjoy these lines from his work 'Ode to a Cat'.

but the cat
only wants to be a cat
and any cat is a cat
from his whiskers to his tail

13 July

Japanese writer Tomoyuki Hoshino was born on this day in 1965. Today's cat is Soccer, the little black-and-white cat from his short story 'We, the Children of Cats'.

Soccer, this little cat marked just like a soccer ball who'd shown up on the veranda during the France World Cup, had a habit of ignoring Masako and running up to me. It always irritated her.

14 July

Today's cat is a stray who makes a brief but poignant appearance in Jeffrey Eugenides' book *The Virgin Suicides*, in which a group of anonymous teenage boys narrate the story of the Lisbon sisters, who are, to them, as fascinating, unknowable and unattainable as cats.

Behind her, on the wall, a shadow swelled. She turned abruptly, then smiled as a stray cat we'd never seen before climbed into her lap. She hugged its unresponsive body until the animal struggled free (that's one more thing we have to include: right up to the end, Lux loved the stray cat. It ran off then, out of this report.)

15 JULY

Author Iris Murdoch was born on this day in 1919. She adored cats, and they sometimes appeared in her work, perhaps most memorably the peculiar Montrose, a tabby who stalks the pages of her 1968 novel *The Nice and the Good*.

Montrose was a large cocoa-coloured tabby animal with golden eyes, a square body, rectangular legs and an obstinate self-absorbed disposition, concerning whose intelligence fierce arguments raged among the children. Tests of Montrose's sagacity were constantly being devised, but there was some uncertainty about the interpretation of the resultant data since the twins were always ready to return to first principles and discuss whether cooperation with the human race was a sign of intelligence at all. Montrose had one undoubted talent, which was that he could at will make his sleek hair stand up on end, and transform himself from a smooth stripey cube into a fluffy sphere. This was called 'Montrose's bird look'.

16 July

As we saw on 20 January, 10 March and 4 July, cats popped up from time to time in the writings of Henry David Thoreau. In the extract below, his biographer Joseph Wood Krutch muses on this, seeming to make a reference to a Rudyard Kipling story (see 30 December).

With the exception of cats, of whom he was extremely fond, he neither at this time nor at any other kept pets, partly no doubt because he himself wanted to be nobody's pet except in so far as he could be, like a cat, one who walked by himself.

– Henry David Thoreau

17 July

On this day in 1941, Virginia Woolf's *Between the Acts* was published, its publication coming just a few months after her death. Today's cat comes from within the book's pages: Sung-Yen, or Sunny to the kitchen staff.

[A] very fine yellow cat [...] rose majestically from the basket chair and advanced superbly to the table, winding the fish.

[...] The cat rubbed itself this way, that way against the table legs, against [Mrs Sands'] legs. She would save a slice for Sunny – his drawing-room name Sung-Yun had undergone a kitchen change into Sunny.

18 July

American journalist and author Hunter S Thompson was born on this day in 1937. He owned two Siamese cats named Caesar and Pele. His widow, Anita, described them as 'Hunter's babies'.

Weird behavior is natural in smart children, like curiosity is to a kitten.

– Kingdom of Fear

19 July

Today is the birthday of Australian writer Garth Nix. To celebrate, today's cat is the white-furred and green-eyed Mogget, a 'strange cat-being' from Nix's Old Kingdom books who wears a rather fetching red collar.

Mogget, the Abhorsen's cat-shaped familiar, was bound by Ranna, the Sleepbringer, first of the seven bells. He had woken only five or six times in nearly twenty years, on three of those occasions to steal and eat fish caught by Touchstone.

– Lirael

20 July

On this day in 1969, Neil Armstrong and Buzz Aldrin landed on the Moon. To mark the anniversary, today's cat is Minnaloushe, from W B Yeats's poem 'The Cat and the Moon'.

The cat went here and there
And the moon spun round like a top,
And the nearest kin of the moon
The creeping cat looked up.
Black Minnaloushe stared at the moon,
For wander and wail as he would
The pure cold light in the sky
Troubled his animal blood.
Minnaloushe runs in the grass,
Lifting his delicate feet.
Do you dance, Minnaloushe, do you dance?
When two close kindred meet
What better than call a dance?
Maybe the moon may learn,
Tired of that courtly fashion,
A new dance turn.

21 July

Writer and famed cat-lover Ernest Hemingway was born on this day in 1899. During his life he owned many dozens of cats, including a polydactyl or six-toed cat named Snow White, who was given to him by a ship's captain. Descendants of his cats live on at the Hemingway Museum in Key West, Florida, which is now home to almost 60 felines, many of whom share the polydactyl trait.

22 July

On this day in 1997, *The Subtle Knife*, the second book in Philip Pullman's His Dark Materials trilogy, was published. Although the daemons that accompany each character in Lyra's universe can take cat form, today's cat, Moxie, is a real feline, who belongs to a young boy named Will.

As Will came round the corner, his cat Moxie rose up from her favourite spot under the still-living hydrangea and stretched before greeting him with a soft miaow and butting her head against his leg.

23 July

Writer Raymond Chandler was born on this day in 1888. In his honour, today's cat is Taki, his beloved pet, who often pops up in his letters – like this one, which Chandler wrote to Charles Morton in March 1945.

A man named Inkstead took some pictures of me for *Harper's Bazaar* a while ago […] and one of me holding my secretary in my lap came out very well indeed. […] The secretary, I should perhaps add, is a black Persian cat, 14 years old, and I call her that because she has been around me ever since I began to write, usually sitting on the paper I wanted to use or the copy I wanted to revise…

24 July

Alexandre Dumas, author of *The Count of Monte Cristo* and *The Three Musketeers*, was born on this day in 1802. He is said to have owned three cats: Mysouff I, Mysouff II, and Le Docteur. In Andrew Lang's 1904 story collection *The Animal Story Book*, he shares a tale from Dumas about one of these felines.

We had a cat in those days whose name was Mysouff. This cat had missed his vocation – he ought to have been a dog. Every morning I started for my office at half-past nine, and came back every evening at half-past five. Every morning Mysouff followed me to the corner of a particular street, and every evening I found him in the same street, at the same corner, waiting for me. Now the curious thing was that on the days when I had found some amusement elsewhere, and was not coming home to dinner, it was no use to open the door for Mysouff to go and meet me. Mysouff, in the attitude of the serpent with its tail in its mouth, refused to stir from his cushion. On the other hand, the days I did come, Mysouff would scratch at the door until someone opened it for him. My mother was very fond of Mysouff; she used to call him her barometer.

25 July

She is a cat with a burning tail, an ant under a microscope, a fly about to lose its wings to the curious plucking fingers of a third-grader on a rainy day, a game for bored children with no bodies and the whole universe at their feet.

– Stephen King, *Under the Dome*

26 July

Writer and philosopher Aldous Huxley was born on this day in 1894. Please enjoy some wise words on writing and cats from a piece he wrote for *Vanity Fair* in September 1930.

If you want to be a psychological novelist and write about human beings, the best thing you can do is keep a pair of cats.

27 July

On this day in 1872, poet Emily Dickinson wrote the following in a letter:

That was a lovely letter of F's. It put the cat to playing and the kettle to purring and two or three birds in plush teams reined nearer the window.

– *The Letters of Emily Dickinson*

28 July

Children's writer and illustrator Beatrix Potter was born on this day in 1866. Today's cat is Tabitha Twitchit, the mother of Miss Moppet and Tom Kitten (see 1 September). She features in several of Potter's stories, and is mentioned as a rival shopkeeper in 'The Tale of Ginger and Pickles'.

29 July

Writer Don Marquis was born on this day in 1878. His is most famous for creating the characters of Archy and Mehitabel – a cockroach and an alley cat, respectively. Mehitabel believes she is a reincarnation of Cleopatra, but:

that was a long time ago
and one must not be
surprised if mehitabel
has forgotten some of her
more regal manners

– Archy and Mehitabel

30 JULY

Emily Brontë was born on this day in 1818. The author of *Wuthering Heights* was a dedicated cat-lover, and the Brontë family owned two cats, Tom and Tiger. In her essay 'The Cat', Emily wrote:

I can say with sincerity that I like cats; also I can give very good reasons why those who despise them are wrong.

A cat is an animal who has more human feelings than almost any other being. We cannot sustain a comparison with the dog, it is infinitely too good; but the cat, although it differs in some physical points, is extremely like us in disposition.

31 JULY

On this day in 1954, a short story written by John Steinbeck (see 27 February) was published in the French newspaper *Le Figaro*. It was written in French, and titled 'Les Puces Symapthiques', or 'The Amiable Fleas'. More than fifty years later, it was published in English for the first time. Unlike some of Steinbeck's more hard-hitting works, the story has a gentle tone. It focuses on the chef Monsieur Amité and his loyal cat Apollo, who assists the chef in the kitchen by tasting the food.

AUGUST

August is a month where everything seems to slow down a little; the days are long and languid, and it's often too warm to do much of anything except loll about. In other words, it's a good month to be a cat. (Sadly, if you're reading this, you are probably a human, and therefore no doubt have to do human things like going to work and doing the grocery shopping. My sympathies.)

This month we'll be spending time with some poetic cats, thanks to Percy Bysshe Shelley, Lord Tennyson and Hal Summers (see 4, 6 and 18 August, respectively), along with a few rather spookier ones in the work of Edgar Allan Poe (see 19 August) and H P Lovecraft (see 20 August).

1 August

Pulitzer Prize-winning American poet Theodore Roethke
died on this day in 1963. In his memory, here are a few cat-
centric lines from his poem 'Praise to the End!'.

> The stones were sharp,
> The wind came at my back;
> Walked along the highway,
> Mincing like a cat.

2 August

Children's book writer James Howe was born on this day
in 1946. He is best known for the Bunnicula series, which
he created with his wife Deborah. The books feature the
Monroe family, and are narrated by Harold, the family dog.
Their home is shared by Chester, an orange tabby with whom
Harold shares an easy friendship. Their lives are turned upside
down, however, when the Monroe children bring home a
rabbit – one that Chester is convinced is a vampire.

> My friend Chester was curled up on the brown velvet
> armchair, which years ago he'd staked out as his own.
> I saw that once again he'd covered the whole seat with
> his cat hair, and I chuckled to myself, picturing the scene
> tomorrow. (Next to grasshoppers, there is nothing that
> frightens Chester more than the vacuum cleaner.)

3 August

English poet and writer Rupert Brooke was born on this day in 1887.

Cities, like cats, will reveal themselves at night.

– Letters from America

4 August

Poet Percy Bysshe Shelley was born on this day in 1792. One of his earliest surviving poems, thought to have been written when he was a boy, is 'A Cat in Distress'.

But this poor little cat
Only wanted a rat,
To stuff out its own little maw;
And it were as good
SOME people had such food,
To make them HOLD THEIR JAW!

5 August

Today's cat is the terrifying Tsarmina Greeneyes, the antagonist of Brian Jacques's book *Mossflower*, part of his hugely popular Redwall series.

'All the land belongs to me,' Tsarmina said imperiously. 'I am Tsarmina, Queen of Kotir and Mossflower. These mice are escaped prisoners. Give them to me now, and I will not punish you.'

6 August

Poet Lord Tennyson was born on this day in 1809. To mark his birthday, today's cats are from his poem 'The Owl' – admittedly only a walk-on part (or perhaps stalk-on?), but the poem would be poorer without them.

When cats run home and light is come,
And dew is cold upon the ground,
And the far-off stream is dumb,
And the whirring sail goes round,
And the whirring sail goes round;
Alone and warming his five wits,
The white owl in the belfry sits.

When merry milkmaids click the latch,
And rarely smells the new-mown hay,
And the cock hath sung beneath the thatch
Twice or thrice his roundelay,
Twice or thrice his roundelay;
Alone and warming his five wits,
The white owl in the belfry sits.

7 August

Today's cat is a truly literary kitty: not only is it described by legendary poet Emily Dickinson, but she also compares it to a member of the Brontë family in this letter written to her cousins in August 1876.

> Vinnie [Dickinson's sister] has a new pussy the colour of Branwell Brontë's hair. She thinks it a little 'lower than the angels', and I concur with her. You remember my ideal cat has always a huge rat in its mouth, just going out of sight.

In a later letter to her sister, dated August 1879, it appears yet another new cat has been acquired:

> Vinnie has a new pussy that catches a mouse an hour. We call her the 'minute hand'.

8 August

Today is International Cat Day, a day to celebrate and appreciate our feline friends. Perhaps author and journalist, Caitlin Moran puts it best:

> [A] cat is a place where you put all the feelings you can't share with humans.
>
> – 'A Death in the Family'

9 AUGUST

Finnish author Tove Jansson was born on this day in 1914. Although she is best known for her Moomin book series, Jansson also wrote for adults, and today's cat is Ma Petite (known as Moppy) from her novel *The Summer Book*.

Moppy was carried around to all the pleasant places a cat might like, but he only glanced at them and walked away. He was flattened with hugs, endured them politely and climbed back into the dish box. He was entrusted with burning secrets and merely averted his yellow gaze. Nothing in the world seemed to interest this cat except food and sleep.

10 AUGUST

In a piece for the Guardian published on this day in 2019, Jessie Burton, author of the bestselling novel *The Miniaturist*, wrote: 'My cat Margot is my constant writing companion.'

11 August

Enid Blyton was born on this day in 1897. Her best-known animal might be Timmy the dog from her Famous Five books, but another fivesome created by Blyton were the Five Find-Outers. In *The Mystery of the Disappearing Cat*, this team had to make use of their best detective skills to find out what had had happened to Lady Candling's prized Siamese cat, Dark Queen.

12 August

Physicist Erwin Schrödinger was born on this day in 1887. He is perhaps best known (among non-physicists, at least) for the thought experiment commonly known as 'Schrödinger's Cat', so please enjoy a few lines from a short story of the same name by Ursula K Le Guin (see also 21 October).

A cat has arrived, interrupting my narrative. It is a striped yellow tom with white chest and paws. He has long whiskers and yellow eyes. I never noticed before that cats had whiskers above their eyes; is that normal? There is no way to tell. As he has gone to sleep on my knee, I shall proceed.

13 AUGUST

Author H G Wells died on this day in 1946. He is said to have had a cat named Mr Peter Wells. In honour of both cat and writer, here is a quote from H G Wells's 1926 novel *The World of William Clissold*.

> The cat, which is a solitary beast, is single-minded and goes its way along, but the dog, like his master, is confused in his mind.

14 AUGUST

Another visit with Behemoth the cat, of *The Master and Margarita* fame. As well as enjoying unusual snacks, like pineapple with salt and pepper, and oysters topped with mustard and grapes, the cat is able to turn champagne into brandy, and serves drinks with finesse.

> 'Noblesse oblige,' remarked the cat, and poured some transparent liquid into a wineglass for Margarita.
> 'Is that vodka?' asked Margarita weakly.
> The cat gave a little jump on his chair in resentment.
> 'For pity's sake, my Queen,' he wheezed, 'would I really permit myself to pour vodka for a lady? This is pure alcohol!'

– Mikhail Bulgakov

15 August

Swedish writer Stieg Larsson was born on this day in 1954. Today's cat is Tjorven, the stray cat from his novel *The Girl with the Dragon Tattoo* who 'adopts' the main character, Mikael Blomkvist.

> Around 7:00 he heard a loud meowing at the front door. A reddish-brown cat slipped swiftly past him into the warmth.
>
> 'Wise cat,' he said.
>
> The cat sniffed around the guest house for a while. Mikael poured some milk into a dish, and his guest lapped it up. Then the cat hopped on to the kitchen bench and curled up. And there she stayed.

16 August

Writer Charles Bukowski was born on this day in 1920. Throughout his life, he owned many cats – including one named Butch van Gough Artaud Bukowski.

17 AUGUST

George Orwell's *Animal Farm* was published on this day in 1945. While the behaviour of some of the animals grows ever more human (and corrupt) throughout the story, the cat remains consistently and delightfully cat-like.

And the behaviour of the cat was somewhat peculiar. It was soon noticed that when there was work to be done the cat could never be found. She would vanish for hours on end, and then reappear at meal-times, or in the evening after work was over, as though nothing had happened. But she always made such excellent excuses, and purred so affectionately, that it was impossible not to believe in her good intentions.

18 AUGUST

Today's cat is the beloved pet of English poet Hal Summers, who was born on this day in 1911 (the poet, that is, not the cat). His poem 'My Old Cat', written about the death of his feline companion, appeared in a collection of Britain's best-loved poems of the twentieth century.

My old cat is dead,
Who would butt me with his head.
He had the sleekest fur.
He had the blackest purr.

19 August

On this day in 1843, Edgar Allan Poe's short story 'The Black Cat' was first published in the *Saturday Evening Post*. Among the most famous of Poe's chilling tales, the story concerns a pet cat belonging to the narrator. Named Pluto, the cat is a 'remarkably large and beautiful animal, entirely black, and sagacious to an astonishing degree'.

After being bitten by the cat, the narrator cuts out one of its eyes in a terrible rage, then later, descending into madness, kills the cat by hanging it.

Of course, Poe never lets a bad deed go unpunished. That night, the narrator's home is destroyed in a blaze – except one wall, upon which appears the image of a huge cat with a rope around its neck.

Later, 'in a den of more than infamy', he spots 'a black cat – a very large one – fully as large as Pluto', and decides to adopt it. Sadly, he soon comes to hate this cat, too (he really should stop getting cats), and tries to kill it with an axe – accidentally slaughtering his wife in the process when she rushes to the cat's aid. He hurriedly hides his wife's body by walling up her corpse in the basement – and then realizes the cat is missing. When police arrive to search the house, they hear the cat meowing from behind a wall and knock it down, discovering his crime in the process.

20 AUGUST

H P Lovecraft, whom we met very briefly on 6 June, was born on this day in 1890. Here are a few lines from his unsettling short story 'The Cats of Ulthar'.

It is said that in Ulthar, which lies beyond the river Skai, no man may kill a cat; and this is I can verily believe as I gaze upon him who sitteth burring before the fire. For the cat is cryptic, and close to strange things men cannot see.

21 AUGUST

Today's cat is Homer, beloved pet of American author Gwen Cooper and the subject of her book *Homer's Odyssey: A Fearless Feline Tale, or How I Learned about Love and Life with a Blind Wonder Cat*. Homer died on this day in 2013, at the grand old age of sixteen.

Every leap Homer took was a leap of faith. Homer was living proof of the adage that fortune favours the brave, that just because you couldn't see the light at the end of the tunnel didn't mean it wasn't there.

22 August

Author Ray Bradbury was born on this day in 1920. He adored cats, and is said to have owned twenty-two. In his short story 'The Cat's Pajamas', two strangers stumble across a seemingly abandoned cat in the road – and both want to take it home.

'Let go of my cat!'
   'Since when was it yours?'
   'I got here first.'
   'It was a tie.'
   'Wasn't.'
   'Was.'
   He pulled at the back and she at the front and suddenly the cat meowed.

23 August

Today's cat is Zorba, the somewhat reluctant hero of Luis Sepulveda's *The Story of a Seagull and the Cat Who Taught Her to Fly*. The big black cat leads a contented existence at the port, until one day he comes across a gull who has been caught up in an oil slick. Before she dies, she entrusts him with her egg – and asks him to raise the chick, and teach it to fly.

24 August

Jorge Luis Borges was born on this day in 1899. He is said to have had a cat named Beppo – perhaps this is who he was thinking of when he wrote his poem 'To a Cat'.

...in the moonlight, you are that panther
we catch sight of from afar.

25 August

Today's cat is a skinny street cat who makes a brief appearance in Susan Meissner's historical novel *As Bright as Heaven*, and in doing so (perhaps inadvertently) saves the life of a baby boy.

I never would have heard the baby if I hadn't followed the cat to the street corner and the front window of the row house hadn't been broken.

The infant's little cries were like the yowls newborn kittens make or a creaky step at the top of the stairs or a little bird in a far-off tree.

26 August

Today is International Dog Day. Mentioning this in a book devoted to the literary cat may seem at best irrelevant and at worst like sacrilege, but it allows us to enjoy this passage from the essay 'Cat and Dog', written by Czech writer and playwright Karel Čapek, and featured in his collection *Intimate Things*.

A cat will play at your instigation; but she can play alone as well. She plays for her own enjoyment, in a self-contained way, with no desire to share. Shut her up alone, and a ball, a fringe, or a lopped piece of string is enough to make her give herself up to silent and graceful sport. [...] She will play beside the bed of a corpse. She will play hide-and-seek with the border of its coverlet. A dog would not do a thing like that. Puss amuses herself on her own. A dog likes to amuse his companion. Puss is only interested in herself. [...] Perhaps that is why she never gives herself up to her play wildly and passionately, to the point of perspiring self-forgetfulness, like a dog. It is always a little beneath her; she always seems to condescend benevolently and somewhat disdainfully when she plays. A dog plays with his whole heart, while a cat only does it lightly, out of caprice.

27 August

Fredrik Backman's novel *A Man Called Ove* was first published on this day in 2012. It tells the story of Ove, a lonely and grumpy widower, who gradually softens and opens up thanks to the efforts of his new neighbours – and a stray cat who keeps showing up.

It was five to six in the morning when Ove and the Cat met for the first time. The cat instantly disliked Ove exceedingly. The feeling was very much reciprocated.

[...] The cat sat with a nonchalant expression in the middle of the footpath that ran between the houses. It had half a tail and only one ear. Patches of fur were missing here and there as if someone had pulled it out in handfuls. Not a very impressive feline.

28 August

Canadian writer Robertson Davies was born on this day in 1913. To mark his birthday, today's cat is Tiger from his book *The Diary of Samuel Marchbanks.*

Seriously disappointed in my kitten Tiger today. During the evening a mouse climbed up through a cold-air grating near my chair and surveyed the room with satisfaction. Aha, I thought, and fetched Tiger, who was sleeping elsewhere. I put her down by the grating, but she immediately climbed up on a sofa and went back to sleep.

29 AUGUST

American poet and essayist Oliver Wendell Holmes Sr was born on this day in 1809. His essay collection *The Autocrat of the Breakfast-Table* includes the following observation:

> I never saw an author in my life—saving, perhaps, one—that did not purr as audibly as a full-grown domestic cat, (Felis Catus, Linn.,) on having his fur smoothed in the right way by a skilful hand.

30 AUGUST

Famed New York City cat veterinarian and writer Louis J Camuti was born on this day in 1893. He spent much of his career caring for the cats of New York, and wrote two books about his experiences: *Park Avenue Vet* and *All My Patients Are Under the Bed: Memoirs of a Cat Doctor.*

> Work – other people's work – is an intolerable idea to a cat. Can you picture cats herding sheep or agreeing to pull a cart? They will not inconvenience themselves to the slightest degree.

31 AUGUST

Confront a cat with something he has never seen before and his first reaction will almost invariably be not one of fear but of curiosity.

– Michael Joseph, Cat's Company

SEPTEMBER

I t's back-to-school time, which means shiny shoes and new pencil cases, and cats breathing a sigh of relief as the homes that have been full of children over the summer holidays empty out and become their quiet kingdoms once more.

This month we'll be meeting a few rather less loveable cats, including Ginger from C S Lewis's *The Last Battle*, Lady Jane from Charles Dickens's *Bleak House* and Buttercup from Suzanne Collins's *The Hunger Games* (see 4, 12 and 14 September respectively), as well as Stephen King's 'The Cat from Hell' (see 21 September). Of course, as true cat-lovers, we adore all felines, including the less beautiful (and possibly demonic) ones. However, we will also be spending some time with Colette's Saha (see 27 September), who is probably the embodiment of beauty in the cat world.

1 September

Today's cat is another of Beatrix Potter's creations: Tom Kitten, son of Tabitha Twitchit (see 28 July). The mischievous Tom infuriates his mother after she dresses him nicely as the family have friends coming over, only for Tom to head out to play, getting himself dirty and losing his clothes to a family of passing ducks in the process.

2 September

American author Cleveland Amory was born on this day in 1917. He wrote three books about his pet cat Polar Bear (see also 25 December),which were gathered together in a collection called *The Compleat Cat*.

As anyone who has ever been around a cat for any length of time well knows, cats have enormous patience with the limitations of the human mind.

– Cleveland Amory, *The Cat Who Came for Christmas*

3 September

Today we return our attention to Robertson Davies's Tiger, whom we last met on 28 August.

Tiger is not better, so I took her to the veterinary this evening. He diagnosed her case as one of garbage-eating [...]. He gave me some pills for her, and also demonstrated the proper way to give pills to a cat [...] I decided that I would use the alternative method, which is to powder the pill and slip it slyly into the cat's food [...]
'A cat is no fool, and she may resent this,' [the vet] said.
– Robertson Davies, *The Diary of Samuel Marchbanks*

4 September

The Last Battle by C S Lewis was published on this day in 1956. Along with the famous lion Aslan (who we will be revisiting on 16 October), the book features a rather less admirable feline – Ginger the tomcat.

'As cunning a tale, Sire, as ever was devised,' said Poggin. 'It was the Cat, Ginger, who told it, and most likely made it up too. This Ginger, Sure – oh, he's a sly-boots if ever a cat was.'

5 SEPTEMBER

I tell David about the fox I saw with a grey body and a red head, and he tells me about his aunt's Siamese cat that yowls just for the pure joy of making noise.

– Phyllis Reynolds Naylor, *Shiloh*

6 SEPTEMBER

Today's cat is another of the big variety: Richard Parker, the tiger from Yann Martel's *Life of Pi*. In the book, a young boy named Pi finds himself stranded on a lifeboat following a shipwreck, with only zoo animals (including Richard Parker) for company. It's possible that Martel named the tiger after real-life cabin boy Richard Parker, who was part of a four-man crew cast adrift at sea after their yacht the *Mignonette* was wrecked. Sadly for young Richard, the rest of his crew killed and ate him after several weeks drifting at sea. They were later rescued, and were brought ashore at Falmouth in the UK on this day in 1884.

A part of me did not want Richard Parker to die at all, because if he died I would be left alone with despair, a foe even more formidable than a tiger. If I still had the will to live, it was thanks to Richard Parker. He kept me from thinking too much about my family and my tragic circumstances. He pushed me to go on living. I hated him for it, yet at the same time I was grateful. I am grateful It's the plain truth: without Richard Parker, I wouldn't be alive today to tell you my story.

7 September

Poet Edith Sitwell was born on this day in 1887. Something of an eccentric, she was known for giving interviews in bed and her absolute devotion to cats. She once declared, with great certainty: 'All poets love cats.'

8 September

On this day in 2004, Susanna Clarke's novel *Jonathan Strange & Mr Norrell* was published in the US. Today's cat is one that features in a brief footnote in this lengthy tale.

He had once found himself in a room with Lady Bessborough's long-haired white cat. He happened to be dressed in an immaculate black coat and trousers, and was therefore thoroughly alarmed by the cat's stalking round and round and making motions as if it proposed to sit on him. He waited until he believed himself to be unobserved, then he picked it up, opened a window and tossed it out. Despite falling three storeys to the ground, the cat survived, but one of its legs was never quite right afterwards and it always evinced the greatest dislike to gentlemen in black clothes.

9 September

What a luxury a cat is, the moments of shocking and startling pleasure in a day, the feel of the beast, the soft sleekness under your palm, the warmth when you wake on a cold night, the grace and charm even in a quite ordinary workaday puss. Cat walks across your room, and in that lonely stalk you see leopard or even panther, or it turns its head to acknowledge you and the yellow blaze of those eyes tells you what an exotic visitor you have here, in this household friend.

– Doris Lessing, 'The Old Age of El Magnifico'

10 SEPTEMBER

Today marks the birthday of artist and writer Philip Gilbert Hamerton, who was born on this day in 1834. In his book *Chapters on Animals*, a collection of his musings and observations on the natural world, he notes:

Of all animals that we can have in a room with us, the cat is the least disturbing. Dogs bring so much dirt into houses that many ladies have a positive horror of them; squirrels leap about in a manner highly dangerous to the ornaments of a drawing-room; whilst monkeys are so incorrigibly mischievous that it is impossible to tolerate them [...]. But you may have a cat in the room with you without anxiety about anything but eatables. He will rob a dish if he can get at it, but he will not, except by the rarest of accidents, displace a sheet of paper or upset an inkstand. The presence of a cat is positively soothing to a student [...]. It is agreeable to feel that you are not absolutely alone, and it seems to you, as you work, as if the cat took care that all her movements should be noiseless, purely out of consideration for your comfort. Then, if you have time to caress her, you know that there will be purring responses, and why inquire too closely into the sincerity of her gratitude?

11 SEPTEMBER

Jack Kerouac's novel *Big Sur* was published on this day in 1962. To mark the occasion, today's cat is the one and only Tyke, whose death is heartbreakingly described in the book. Here Kerouac describes happier memories of his beloved cat.

I loved Tyke with all my heart, he was my baby boy who as a kitten just slept in the palm of my hand with his little head hanging down, or just purring, for hours, just as long as I held him that way, walking or sitting—He was like a floppy fur wrap round my wrist, I just twist him around my wrist or drape him and he just purred and purred and even when he got big I still held him that way[.]

12 September

On this day in 1853, the final part of Charles Dickens's epic novel *Bleak House* came out, having been published in serial form beginning in March 1852. In its honour, today's cat is the inimitable Lady Jane (sometimes referred to as 'Ya Brimstone Beast'), a sharp-eyed and sharper-clawed feline belonging to Mr Krook. In the extract below, Miss Flite explains that she can't open the window to her apartment because she keeps birds, and Lady Jane will surely pounce.

The birds began to stir and chirp.

'I cannot admit the air freely,' said the little old lady; the room was close, and would have been the better for it; 'because the cat you saw downstairs – called Lady Jane – is greedy for their lives. She crouches on the parapet outside for hours and hours. I have discovered,' whispering mysteriously, 'that her natural cruelty is sharpened by a jealous fear of their regaining their liberty. In consequence of the judgement I expect being shortly given. She is sly, and full of malice. I half-believe, sometimes, that she is no cat, but the wolf of the old saying. It is so very difficult to keep her from the door.'

13 September

Roald Dahl was born on this day in 1916. Although he is probably best remembered for his children's books, today's cat is from one of his stories for adults: 'Edward the Conqueror'. The story concerns a couple, Edward and Louisa, who take in a stray cat – only for Louisa to become convinced that the cat is the classical musician Liszt reincarnated. Cat-lovers, be warned – the ending is not for the faint-hearted.

Every time I play Liszt, he gets all excited and comes running over to sit on the stool beside me. But only for Liszt, and nobody can teach a cat the difference between Liszt and Schumann.

14 September

On this day in 2008, Suzanne Collins's novel *The Hunger Games* was first published – and the world got a new heroine. Impressive as Katniss Everdeen is, however, today we are focusing on Buttercup, the grouchy pet cat belonging to Katniss's little sister, Prim.

Sitting at Prim's knees, guarding her, is the world's ugliest cat. Mashed-in nose, half of one ear missing, eyes the colour of rotting squash. Prim named him Buttercup, insisting that his muddy yellow coat matched the bright flower. He hates me. Or at least distrusts me.

15 September

As London Fashion Week typically falls around mid-September (as well as in February and June), today's cat is of the well-dressed variety: T S Eliot's Bustopher Jones, an epicurean cat with a taste for the finer things in life. As Eliot notes: 'No commonplace mousers have such well-cut trousers.'

It's called the catwalk for a reason, you know.

16 September

'We sleep researchers like cats, you know; they sleep a lot!'
– Ursula K Le Guin, *The Lathe of Heaven*

17 September

Today's cat is from a poem (titled simply 'Poem') written by American poet and physician William Carlos Williams, who was born on this day in 1883. The poem's short lines, made up of just one, two or three words, neatly echo the precise way a cat manoeuvres when it's picking its way across a crowded surface:

> [...] first the right
> forefoot
> carefully then the hind
> stepped down [...]

18 September

English writer and lexicographer Samuel Johnson was born on this day in 1709. While he dedicated much of his life to the beauty and meaning of words, he was equally devoted to his cat, Hodge, who has since been immortalized in the form of a statue outside Johnson's former home in Gough Square, London. Johnson's biographer James Boswell noted that Johnson described Hodge as 'a very fine cat, a very fine cat indeed', and observed:

> I never shall forget the indulgence with which he treated Hodge, his cat: for whom he himself used to go out and buy oysters, lest the servants having that trouble should take a dislike to the poor creature.

> – *The Life of Samuel Johnson*

19 September

Today's cat is Fritti Tailchaser, star of *Tailchaser's Song* by Tad Williams, a novel set in a world where cats have their own culture, are deeply suspicious of the strange species they call 'M'an'.

He was deep in a dream of leaping and flying when he felt an unusual tingling in his whiskers. Fritti Tailchaser, hunterchild of the Folk, came suddenly awake and sniffed the air. Ears pricked and whiskers flared straight, he sifted the evening breeze.

20 September

Poet and novelist Stevie Smith was born on this day in 1902. To mark the day, today's cat is the star of her poem 'The Singing Cat', which describes a 'little captive cat' on a busy train who begins to miaow and 'sing' 'in plaintive melody', to the delight of the other passengers.

He lifteth up his innocent paw
Upon her breast he clingeth
And everybody cries, Behold
The cat, the cat that singeth.

21 September

American writer and king of horror Stephen King was born on this day in 1947. To celebrate his birthday, here is an excerpt from his short story 'The Cat from Hell', in which a hitman is hired to take on an unusual target: a cat. It might seem like this would be an easy job, but it turns out the cat is determined not to go quietly.

For a moment Halston and the cat stared at each other. It was a strange moment for Halston, who was an unimaginative man with no superstitions. For that one moment as he knelt on the floor with the gun pointed, he felt that he knew this cat, although if he had ever seen one with such unusual markings he surely would have remembered.

22 September

Today's cat is Pitty Sing, from Flannery O'Connor's short story 'A Good Man is Hard to Find'. The story describes a family on an ill-fated road trip, with Pitty Sing having been snuck into the car by the grandmother, who doesn't want to leave him alone while they're gone. Unfortunately, the cat gets startled and leaps out of its hiding place, causing an accident.

> The car turned over and landed right-side-up in a gulch off the side of the road. Bailey remained in the driver's seat with the cat – grey-striped with a broad white face and an orange nose – clinging to his neck like a caterpillar.

23 September

On this day in 1813, beloved novelist Jane Austen wrote to her sister Cassandra:

> Let me know when you begin the new tea, and the new white wine. My present elegancies have not yet made me indifferent to such matters. I am still a cat if I see a mouse.

24 September

After celebrating his birthday just a few days ago, we're back in the spooky world of Stephen King, as his novel *Doctor Sleep*, a sequel to his famous tale *The Shining*, was published on this day in 2013. The book features a grey cat named Azreel, or Azzie for short, who lives in a hospice and has the strange power of being able to tell when someone is about to die.

[Azzie] never went into the guest rooms unless one of the guests was dying.

Then he would either slip in (if the door was unlatched) or sit outside with his tail curled around his haunches, waowing in a low, polite voice to be admitted. When he was, he would jump up on the guests bed [...] and settle there, purring. If the person so chosen happened to be awake, he or she might stroke the cat. To Dan's knowledge, no one had ever demanded that Azzie be evicted. They seemed to know he was there as a friend.

25 September

Dogs are not like cats, who amusingly tolerate humans only until someone comes up with a tin opener that can be operated with a paw.

– Terry Pratchett, *Men at Arms*

26 September

Poet and playwright T S Eliot was born on this day in 1888 – and no book on literary cats would be complete without reference to his beloved work *Old Possum's Book of Practical Cats*, which was illustrated by Edward Gorey. In Eliot's honour, today's cat is Rum Tum Tugger, a 'Curious Cat':

> For he will do
> As he do do
> And there's no doing anything about it.

Perhaps not so 'curious' after all; that seems to describe most cats.

27 September

Today's cat is Saha, from Colette's novella *La Chatte* (The Cat), a beautiful feline adored by her owner Alain – to the extent that his partner, Camille, grows jealous.

> He had read her like some masterpiece from the day, when on his return from a cat-show, Alain had put down a little five-months-old she-cat on the smooth lawn at Neuilly. He had bought her because of her perfect face, her precocious dignity and her modesty that hoped for nothing beyond the bars of a cage.

28 September

'I'm going to tell you all your faults. Number one: you squeaked twice while Dinah was washing your face this morning. Now you can't deny it, Kitty: I heard you! What's that you say?' (Pretending that the kitten was speaking.) 'Her paw went in your eye? Well, that's your fault, for keeping your eyes open – if you'd shut them tight up, it wouldn't have happened. Number two: you pulled Snowdrop away by the tail just as I had put down the saucer of milk before her! What, you were thirsty, were you? How do you know she wasn't thirsty too? Now for number three: you unwound every bit of the worsted while I wasn't looking!

'That's three faults, Kitty, and you've not been punished for any of them yet. You know I'm saving up all your punishments for Wednesday week – Suppose they saved up all my punishments!' she went on, talking more to herself than the kitten. 'What would they do at the end of a year? I should be sent to prison, I suppose, when the day came.'

– Lewis Carroll, *Through the Looking-Glass, and What Alice Found There*

Spanish writer Miguel de Cervantes was born on this day in 1547. In his honour, today's cats are from a disastrous scene in his epic tale *Don Quixote*, in which the eponymous hero is interrupted in the middle of singing a ballad to the object of his affections by an entire sackful of feline interrupters.

Don Quixote had got so far with his song, to which the duke, the duchess, Altisidora, and nearly the whole household of the castle were listening, when all of a sudden from a gallery above that was exactly over his window they let down a cord with more than a hundred bells attached to it, and immediately after that discharged a great sack full of cats, which also had bells of smaller size tied to their tails. Such was the din of the bells and the squalling of the cats, that though the duke and duchess were the contrivers of the joke they were startled by it, while Don Quixote stood paralysed with fear; and as luck would have it, two or three of the cats made their way in through the grating of his chamber, and flying from one side to the other, made it seem as if there was a legion of devils at large in it. They extinguished the candles that were burning in the room, and rushed about seeking some way of escape; the cord with the large bells never ceased rising and falling; and most of the people of the castle, not knowing what was really the matter, were at their wits' end with astonishment. Don Quixote sprang to his feet, and drawing his sword, began making passes at the grating, shouting out, 'Avaunt, malignant enchanters! avaunt, ye witchcraft-working rabble! I am Don Quixote of La Mancha, against whom your evil machinations avail not nor have any power.' And turning upon the cats that were running about the room, he made several cuts at them. They dashed at the grating and escaped by it, save one that, finding itself hard pressed by the slashes of Don Quixote's sword, flew at his face and held on to his nose tooth and nail, with the pain of which he began to shout his loudest. The duke and duchess hearing this, and guessing what it was, ran with all haste to his room, and as the poor gentleman was striving with all his might to detach the cat from his face, they opened the door with a master-key and went in with lights and witnessed the unequal combat.

30 September

Truman Capote was born on this day in 1924. In his honour, today's cat is the nameless 'red tiger-striped tom', feline companion of Holly Golightly in *Breakfast at Tiffany's*.

If I had a real-life place that made me feel like Tiffany's, then I'd buy some furniture and give the cat a name.

OCTOBER

Autumn is here: the days are getting shorter, the breeze is getting cooler and the leaves are falling from the trees (see 7 April for a very sweet poem about a kitten trying to catch falling leaves, by the way). This month, we'll be meeting some felines with slightly unfortunate names (see 14 and 15 October), as well as the awe-inspiring Aslan (see 16 October).

More than anything, though, October is all about Halloween. For cat-lovers that means witches and their feline familiars, including *Meg and Mog* (see 10 October), *Magpie* and the aunts of *Practical Magic* (see 30 October) and, of course, Graymalkin and the witches of *Macbeth* (see 31 October). There's also space for some ghost stories, vampires and an invisible cat.

1 October

Today's cat is the mischievous Simpkin from Beatrix Potter's 1903 tale *The Tailor of Gloucester*. What with trapping mice under a tea cup and hiding the tailor's buttonhole twist, Simpkin certainly manages to cause chaos.

2 October

'If you shamefully misuse a cat once she will always maintain a dignified reserve toward you afterward. You can never get her full confidence again.'

– attributed to Mark Twain

3 OCTOBER

Author and veterinarian James Herriot was born on this day in 1916. He is best known for his books about working as a vet in a rural practice in Yorkshire. Most of his patients were of the large farmyard variety, and in his book *Cat Stories*, he notes that he was worried he would end up missing cats. But happily, it turns out he was wrong.

There were cats everywhere. Every farm had its cats. They kept the mice away and lived a whole life of their own in those rural places. The are connoisseurs of comfort, and when inspecting the head of a cow I often found a cosy nest of kittens with mother in the hay rack. They were to be seen snuggled between bales of straw or stretched blissfully in sunlit corners because they love warmth, and in the bitter days of winter the warm bonnet of my car was an irresistible attraction.

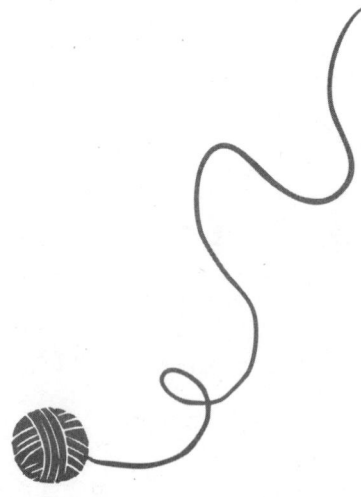

4 OCTOBER

The world has different owners at sunrise. [...] Even your own garden does not belong to you. Rabbits and blackbirds have the lawns; a tortoise-shell cat who never appears in daytime patrols the brick walls, and a golden-tailed pheasant glints his way through the iris spears.

– Anne Morrow Lindbergh, *Listen! The Wind*

5 OCTOBER

Old Possum's Book of Practical Cats by T S Eliot was published on this day in 1939. With cats including Growltiger, Grumbuskin, Lady Griddlebone, the Jellicle Cats and Asparagus (known as Gus), the poems are filled with delight.

See 15 and 26 September, and 12 December.

6 October

Today's cat comes from Clarissa Pinkola Estés's retelling of
'The Ugly Duckling', featured in her book *Women Who Run
With the Wolves*.

> Toward nightfall, [the duckling] came to a poor hovel;
> the door was hanging by a thread, there were more cracks
> than walls. Here lived an old raggedy woman with her
> uncombed cat and her cross-eyed hen. The cat earned
> her keep with the old woman by catching mice. The hen
> earned her keep by laying eggs.

7 October

Zelda Fitzgerald's *Save Me the Waltz* was published on this
day in 1932. While there is only the briefest mention of cats
in the novel, Fitzgerald herself is said to have had cats named
Chat, Chopin and Ezra Pound.

> The unjubilant moon was tarnished with much
> summer use in the salt air and the shadows black and
> communicative. A cat clambered over the balcony. It
> was very hot.

8 OCTOBER

Virginia Woolf's novel *The Waves* was first published on
this day in 1931.

> I want this fire, I want this chair. I want someone to
> sit beside me after the day's pursuit and all its anguish,
> after its listenings, and its waitings, and its suspicions.
> After quarrelling and reconciliation I need privacy – to
> be alone with you, to set this hubbub in order. For I am
> as neat as a cat in my habits.

9 OCTOBER

Japanese writer Jirō Osaragi (real name Kiyohiko Nojiri) was
born on this day in 1897. Known for his historical novels,
he was a renowned cat-lover, and was said to have cared for
and fed at least 500 semi-feral cats at his house in Kamakura.

10 OCTOBER

Children's book author Helen Nicoll was born on 10 October
1937. She is the creator of the Meg and Mog series, featuring the
not-always-very-successful witch Meg and her stripy cat Mog.

11 October

As the nights draw in and we approach Halloween, today's extract comes from Bram Stoker's *Dracula*. In the novel, psychiatrist Dr Seward's patient Renfield has been begging him for a cat. Writing up his notes, the doctor realizes what he wanted it for...

What he desires is to absorb as many lives as he can, and he has laid himself out to achieve it in a cumulative way. He gave many flies to one spider and many spiders to one bird, and then wanted a cat to eat the many birds. What would have been his later steps? It would almost be worth while to complete the experiment.

12 October

Today's cat is Lariflete, one of the feline companions of Armande in Joanne Harris's novel *Chocolat*. The old woman and her cat are devoted to each other.

'I've had her nineteen years. That makes her nearly my age, in cat time.' She made a small clucking sound at the cat, which purred louder. 'I'm supposed to be allergic,' said Armande. 'Asthma or something. I told them that I'd rather choke than get rid of my cats. Though there are some humans I could give up without a second thought.' Lariflete whisker-twitched lazily.

13 OCTOBER

Our feline today is the white cat that finds itself the unfortunate subject of an experiment in H G Wells's 1897 novel *The Invisible Man*. Having created a formula for rendering things invisible, the scientist Griffin tries to use it on the cat – but things don't work out quite as he'd expected, as the formula fails to work on the cat's eyes.

About two, the cat began miaowing about the room. I tried to hush it by talking to it, and then I decided to turn it out. I remember the shock I had when striking a light – there were just the round eyes shining green – and nothing around them. I would have given it milk, but I hadn't any. It wouldn't be quiet, just sat and miaowed at the door. I tried to catch it, with an idea of putting it out of the window, but it wouldn't be caught, it vanished. Then it began miaowing in different parts of the room. At last I opened the window and made a bustle. I suppose it went out at last. I never saw any more of it.

14 October

Today's cat is the rather hilariously named Tits from *The Liar's Dictionary* by Eley Williams. Tits is the office cat, prowling around the desks of the dictionary editors working at Swansby House.

> I had first met Tits during the interview for my current role. He was a rangy, yellow-eyed duffer-moggy with a coat the colour of old toast. His presence as an interviewer ('Ignore the cat at your feet! Please, do sit down!') was not unwelcome.

15 October

Continuing yesterday's theme of cats with unfortunate names, today's feline is Dr Butthole from Patricia Lockwood's award-winning novel *No One is Talking About This*.

> One hundred years ago, her cat might have been called Mittens or Pussywillow. Now her cat was called Dr Butthole. There was no way out of it. 'Dr Butthole,' she called at night, almost in despair, until he trotted to the door with the bright feathers of her dignity clinging to his lips and disappeared in his alternating stripes over the threshold.

16 October

This day in 1950 saw the publication of the children's classic *The Lion, the Witch and the Wardrobe*, which tells the tale of the four Pevensie children, who find their way into the magical yet wintry land of Narnia via a mysterious wardrobe. In an effort to defeat the evil White Witch, they join forces with other characters – including the magnificent lion Aslan, 'the King of the wood and the song of the great Emperor-Beyond-the Sea'.

> [T]he Beavers and the children didn't know what to do or say when they saw [Aslan]. People who have not been in Narnia sometimes think that a thing cannot be good and terrible at the same time. If the children had ever thought so, they were cured of it now. For when they tried to look at Aslan's face they just caught a glimpse of the golden mane and the great, royal, solemn, overwhelming eyes; and then they found they couldn't look at him and went all trembly.

17 October

Although it would seem at first glance that hobbits and cats have a good deal in common – fond of comfortable places, warmth and food – they don't make much of an appearance in J R R Tolkien's *The Hobbit* (although in *Lord of the Rings* there is a brief reference to 'the cats of Queen Berúthiel'). They do, however, have a role of sorts to play in the game of riddles between Bilbo and Gollum.

[…] Bilbo asked another riddle as quick as ever he could, so that Gollum had to get back into his boat and think.

No-legs lay on one-leg, two-legs sat near on three-legs, four-legs got some.

It was not really the right time, but Bilbo was in a hurry. […] 'Fish on a little table, man at table sitting on a stool, the cat has the bones' – that of course is the answer, and Gollum soon gave it.

18 October

Today's cats are Luna and Artemis from Naoko Takeuchi's manga series Sailor Moon. Luna is a talking black cat who serves as an advisor and companion to Usagi, or Sailor Moon, while Artemis is a white cat who supports and guides Minako, or Sailor Venus.

19 OCTOBER

Charlotte Brontë's *Jane Eyre* was first published on this day in 1847. As we have seen, the Brontë family were great cat-lovers, and in one early scene, Brontë uses the presence of a cat to signify calm and domestic comfort as Jane Eyre meets Mrs Fairfax for the first time.

A snug, small room; a round table by a cheerful fire; an arm-chair high-backed and old-fashioned, wherein sat the neatest imaginable little elderly lady, in widow's cap, black silk gown and snowy muslin apron: exactly like what I had fancied Mrs Fairfax, only less stately and milder looking. She was occupied in knitting; a large cat sat demurely at her feet; nothing in short was wanting to complete the beau-ideal of domestic comfort. A more reassuring introduction for a new governess could scarcely be conceived; there was no grandeur to overwhelm, no stateliness to embarrass; and then, as I entered, the old lady got up and promptly and kindly came forward to meet me.

20 October

Canadian politician, writer and suffragist Nellie McClung was born on this day in 1873. As well as nine novels, she wrote a number of non-fiction titles including *In Times Like These*, which featured the observation below:

> In regard to tenacity of life, no old yellow cat has anything on a prejudice. You may kill it with your own hands, bury it deep, and sit on the grave, and behold! the next day, it will walk in at the back door, purring.

21 October

American author Ursula K Le Guin was born on this day in 1929. She is known to have kept cats, including Mother Courage and Lorenzo (Bonzo for short), but today's cat is Pard, the narrator of *My Life So Far*, which Le Guin explained she had 'translated from the feline'.

The aunty human went away and left me with the old queen and an old tom. I was distrustful of him at first, but my fears were groundless. When he sits down he has an excellent thing, a lap. Other humans have them, but his is mine. It is full of quietness and fondness. The old queen sometimes parts hers and says prrt? and I know perfectly well what she means; but I only use one lap, his. What I like to use about her is the place behind her knees on the bed, and the top of her head, which having a kind of fur reminds me a little of my Mother, so sometimes I get on the pillow with it and knead it. This works best when she is asleep.

22 October

Today marks the birth of one of literature's finest cat ladies, Doris Lessing, who was born on this day in 1919. Known for her prize-winning novels, she also devoted herself to her cats, and wrote in detail about their lives, loves and rivalries. In her honour, today's cat is 'grey cat', one of the feline heroines of her non-fiction work *Particularly Cats*.

Grey cat licks my face, delicately, looks briefly out of the window at the night, acknowledging tree, moon, stars, winds, or the amours of other cats from which she is now infinitely removed, then settles down. In the morning, when she wishes me to wake, she crouches on my chest, and pats my face with her paw. Or, if I am on my side, she crouches looking into my face. Soft, soft touches of her paw. I open my eyes. Cat gently pats my eyelids. Cat licks my nose. Cat starts purring, two inches from my face. Cat, then, as I lie pretending to be asleep, delicately bites my nose. I laugh and sit up.

23 October

Lestat trusted no one, as you see. He was like a cat, by his own admission, a lone predator.

– Anne Rice, *Interview with the Vampire*

24 October

Today's cat is William Cat, from Ian McEwan's children's novel *The Daydreamer*, in which a young boy called Peter imagines that he has switched bodies with the family cat.

[Peter] liked to get right down to William's level and put his face up close to the cat's and see how extraordinary it really was, how beautifully nonhuman, with spikes of black hair sprouting in a globe from a tiny face beneath the fur, and the white whiskers with their slight downward curve, and the eyebrow hairs shooting up like radio antennae, and the pale-green eyes with their upright slits, like doors ajar into a world Peter could never enter. As soon as he came close to the cat, the deep rumbling purr would begin, so low and strong that the floor vibrated. Peter knew he was welcome.

25 October

Cats and humans have been partners for over ten thousand years. And what you realise when you've lived with a cat for a long time is that we may think we own them, but that's not the way it is. They simply allow us the pleasure of their company.

– Genki Kawamura, *If Cats Disappeared From the World*

26 October

'I'm not misbehaving, I'm not bothering anyone, I'm mending the Primus,' said the cat with an unfriendly frown, 'and I consider it my duty to warn you that the cat is an ancient and inviolable animal.'

– Mikhail Bulgakov, *The Master and Margarita*

27 October

American poet and writer Sylvia Plath was born on this day in 1932. In her honour, here are a couple of lines from her poem 'Ella Mason and Her Eleven Cats'.

Old Ella Mason keeps cats, eleven at last count,
In her ramshackle house off Somerset Terrace.

28 October

On this day in 1726, Jonathan Swift's *Gulliver's Travels* was published. In the book, the eponymous hero travels to strange and distant lands, including Lilliput, where he is imprisoned by the island's tiny inhabitants, and Brobdingnag, where Gulliver himself is comparatively tiny, and he meets a farmer who is 72 feet tall – and owns a similarly enormous cat.

In the midst of dinner, my mistress's favourite cat leaped into her lap. I heard a noise behind me like that of a dozen stocking-weavers at work; and turning my head, I found it proceeded from the purring of that animal, who seemed to be three times larger than an ox, as I computed by the view of her head, and one of her paws, while her mistress was feeding and stroking her. The fierceness of this creature's countenance altogether discomposed me; though I stood at the farther end of the table, above fifty feet off; and although my mistress held her fast, for fear she might give a spring, and seize me in her talons. But it happened there was no danger, for the cat took not the least notice of me when my master placed me within three yards of her. And as I have been always told, and found true by experience in my travels, that flying or discovering fear before a fierce animal, is a certain way to make it pursue or attack you, so I resolved, in this dangerous juncture, to show no manner of concern. I walked with intrepidity five or six times before the very head of the cat, and came within half a yard of her; whereupon she drew herself back, as if she were more afraid of me: I had less apprehension concerning the dogs, whereof three or four came into the room, as it is usual in farmers' houses; one of which was a mastiff, equal in bulk to four elephants, and another a greyhound, somewhat taller than the mastiff, but not so large.

29 October

Audrey Niffenegger's short story 'Secret Life, With Cats' tells the tale of a woman who starts volunteering at a cat shelter, which is run by a kindly lady named Ruth. It starts out quite cosily, but things soon turn ghostly – it is almost Halloween, after all.

> I slowly developed a rapport with certain cats. My favourites were Lucky, an earless, balding thing who loved to sit in my lap for hours; Madge, a tortoiseshell who bit everyone but me; and Elvis, a fat blond cat who followed me everywhere and loved chewing on my wristwatch band.

30 October

If you cast your mind back to 16 March, you may remember the troupe of cats following young Sally to school at the start of Alice Hoffman's *Practical Magic*. By the end of the novel, Sally is grown up, with two daughters, and only one cat remains.

> The only cat left is Magpie, who is so ancient he gets up only in order to get to his food bowl. The rest of the time he's curled onto a special silk cushion on a kitchen chair. One of Magpie's eyes doesn't open at all anymore, but his good eye is fixed on the turkey, which is cooling on an earthenware platter in the centre of the table.

31 OCTOBER

Today is Halloween, and so our cat is Graymalkin, the familiar of one of the witches in Shakespeare's *Macbeth* (the other familiar mentioned below, Paddock, is a toad).

Thunder and lightning. Enter three WITCHES.

FIRST WITCH:
When shall we three meet again
In thunder, lightning, or in rain?
SECOND WITCH:
When the hurlyburly's done,
When the battle's lost and won.
THIRD WITCH:
That will be ere the set of sun.
FIRST WITCH:
Where the place?
SECOND WITCH:
Upon the heat.
THIRD WITCH:
There to meet Macbeth.
FIRST WITCH:
I come, Graymalkin!
SECOND WITCH:
Paddock calls.
THIRD WITCH:
Anon.
ALL:
Fair is foul, and foul is fair:
Hover through the fog and filthy air.

NOVEMBER

Winter is here, the nights are drawing in and the temperatures are dropping. It's time to light some candles, turn on the heating, seek out your warmest blanket and get cosy, in true cat-like fashion.

We're spending time with some futuristic felines this month, including *Red Dwarf*'s evolved Cat (see 2 November) and the strange purring human-like creatures of *Oryx and Crake* (see 9 November). To balance things out, we'll also be visiting the world of *Little Women* to hang out with the March sisters and their cats (see 15 and 29 November).

Moveable feasts

NATIONAL NOVEL WRITING MONTH: November is National Novel Writing Month (also known as NaNoWriMo). Anyone can take part in this creative writing event: the idea is simply to commit to putting pen to paper every day and writing (or beginning to write) a novel. As we've seen throughout this book, one of the most important tools for successful writing is a cat: every poet, novelist and scholar needs a feline companion. Cats are as essential to writers as pen and paper.

1 November

Terry Pratchett's novel *The Amazing Maurice and His Educated Rodents* was published on this day in 2001. Part of his Discworld series, the novel follows the adventures of the human boy Keith, the titular Maurice, a wise cat, and a group of talking rats known as 'the Clan'.

Maurice watched them argue again. Humans, eh? Think they're lords of creation. Not like us cats. We know we are. Ever see a cat feed a human? Case proven.

2 NOVEMBER

Red Dwarf: Infinity Welcomes Careful Drivers by Rob Grant and Doug Naylor was first published on this day in 1989. The novel is based on their hit TV series *Red Dwarf*, and recounts the adventures of Lister, Rimmer, Kryten and the Cat, a creature that has evolved over millions of years from the pet cat named Frankenstein that Lister smuggled aboard the spaceship before being frozen in stasis.

'So he's a Cat,' said Lister for the fourteenth time.

The Cat took a small portable steam iron out of his pocket and started pressing the sleeve of his jacket.

Outwardly, at least, he was human in appearance – there was a slight flattening of his face; his ears were a little higher on his head; and two of his gleaming upper teeth hung down longer and sharper than the others, so they peeked, whitely, over his lips whenever he grinned. Which he did a lot.

3 November

Although the most significant non-human character in Gabriel García Márquez's novel *Love in the Time of Cholera* is probably Urbino's parrot, there is a cat – and it does not fail to make its presence known, frequently interfering in the love affair between Sara Noriega and Florentino Ariza.

Among many other things that he did not like, he had to resign himself to having the furious cat in bed with them, although Sara Noriega had his claws removed so he would not tear them apart while they made love.

4 NOVEMBER

Today's cat is none other than Church (short for Winston Churchill), the sinister family pet at the heart of Stephen King's novel *Pet Sematary*, which was published on this day in 1983. King has said that the inspiration for the tale came when his real-life pet Smucky was run over. In the novel, Church meets a similar fate – but then, after being buried, he comes home...

He let Church into the house, got his blue dish, and opened a tuna-and-liver cat dinner. As he spooned the gray-brown mess out of the can, Church purred unevenly and rubbed back and forth along Louis's ankles. The feel of the cat caused Louis to break out in gooseflesh, and he had to clench his teeth grimly to keep from kicking him away. His furry sides felt somehow too slick, too thick – in a word, loathsome. Louis found he didn't care if he never touched Church again.

5 NOVEMBER

On Cats, a posthumously published collection of Charles Bukowski's musings on felines, was published on this day in 2015.

If you're feeling bad, you just look at the cats, you'll feel better, because they know that everything is, just as it is. There's nothing to get excited about. They just know. They're saviours. The more cats you have, the longer you live. If you have a hundred cats, you'll live 10 times longer than if you have 10. Someday this will be discovered, and people will have a thousand cats and live for ever. It's truly ridiculous.

6 NOVEMBER

Clara, of course, was all cat. She wore a long brown woollen Jeff Banks dress and a perfect set of false teeth; the dress was backless, the teeth were white, and the overall effect was feline; a panther in an evening dress; where the wall stopped and Clara's skin started was not clear to the naked eye. And like a cat she responded to the dusty sunbeam that was coursing through a high window on to the waiting couples. She warmed her bare back in it, she almost seemed to unfurl.

– Zadie Smith, *White Teeth*

7 November

Austrian zoologist and writer Konrad Lorenz was born on this day in 1903. Here are his expert observations on the differences between cats and dogs.

The whole charm of the dog lies in the depth of friendship and the strength of the spiritual ties with which he has bound himself to man, but the appeal of the cat lies in the very fact that she has formed no close bond with him, that she has the uncompromising independence of a tiger or a leopard while she is hunting in his stables and barns; that she still remains mysterious and remote when she is rubbing herself gently against the legs of her mistress or purring contentedly in front of the fire. The purring cat is, for me, a symbol of the hearthside and the hidden security which it stands for.

8 NOVEMBER

Today's cat is Portia, the feline companion of Barbara, one of the main characters in Zoë Heller's 2003 novel *Notes on a Scandal*.

Portia jumped up and stalked about for a bit, testing out potential sleeping spots with her claws. She committed, finally, to lying heavily – and hotly – across my calves. I set my alarm and turned out the light. Through a gap in the curtains, a moonbeam shone glamorously on Portia, like a spotlight.

9 NOVEMBER

In Margaret Atwood's dystopian novel *Oryx and Crake*, the genius Crake creates a new type of human-like creatures that become known as Crakers. He uses genetic engineering to give them certain traits – including the ability to purr.

Crake had worked for years on the purring. Once he'd discovered that the cat family purred at the same frequency as the ultrasound used on bone fractures and skin lesions and were thus equipped with their own self-healing mechanism, he'd turned himself inside out in the attempt to install that feature.

10 NOVEMBER

Today is World Science Day for Peace and Development. To mark the date, today's cat is F D C Willard, also known as Chester, a Siamese cat whose owner, J H Hetherington, often listed him as co-author (and sometimes even the sole author) of scientific papers. This is said to have come about because Hetherington had mistakenly used the term 'we' in one of his papers, but as a sole author it would have caused his paper to be rejected. Rather than type the whole thing out again, he decided to invent a co-author, and Chester – or F D C Willard – was happy to oblige. (F D stands for *Felis domesticus*, by the way).

11 NOVEMBER

Very few human beings are privileged to know the cat. He does not care whether you like him or not. If you give him food and shelter he will accept it; if not, he will find it for himself. He is a philosopher.

– Michael Joseph, *Cat's Company*

12 November

Let Hercules himself do what he may,
The cat will mew and dog will have his day.

– William Shakespeare, *Hamlet*, Act V, Scene 1

13 November

A cat is better than you are, more honest, more graceful, smarter for her size, and infinitely more beautiful. A cat has the face of a pansy flower, and is just as velvety. A cat holds infinity in her eyes, and your heart in her front paws.

– Leonore Fleischer, *The Cat's Pajamas*

14 November

Charlotte, maddening. Charlotte doing that maddening thing, always stopping to speak to just any cat she's seen in the street, in any street, here, there, in Greece on holiday, anywhere she sees a fucking cat getting down on her haunches and stretching her hand out like Art's not there, like the cats won't want to speak to him anyway even if he is, like the whole world has shifted to just her and some cat she doesn't even know...

– Ali Smith, *Winter*

15 November

In Louisa May Alcott's novel *Little Women*, the March sisters amuse themselves by putting together a weekly newspaper, which they name the *Pickwick Portfolio*. It included the following announcement:

THE PUBLIC BEREAVEMENT

It is our painful duty to record the sudden and mysterious disappearance of our cherished friend, Mrs Snowball Pat Paw. This lovely and beloved cat was the pet of a large circle of warm and admiring friends; for her beauty attracted all eyes, her graces and virtues endeared her to all hearts, and her loss is deeply felt by the whole community.

When last seen, she was sitting at the gate, watching the butcher's cart; and it is feared that some villain, tempted by her charms, basely stole her. Weeks have passed, but no trace of her has been discovered; and we relinquish all hope, tie a black ribbon to her basket, set aside her dish, and weep for her as one lost to us forever.

16 November

If you cast your mind back to 25 April, you might remember William Cowper's poem about his cat and her love of seeking out cosy spots in which to snooze. Here's an extract from a letter he wrote to Lady Hesketh in November 1787, thought to be about that very same cat when she was still just a kitten.

I have a kitten my dear, the drollest of all creatures that ever wore a cat's skin. Her gambols are not to be described, and would be incredible, if they could. In point of size she is likely to be a kitten always, being extremely small of her age; but time, I suppose, that spoils everything, will make her also a cat. You will see her, I hope, before that melancholy period shall arrive, for no wisdom that she may gain by experience and reflection hereafter, will compensate the loss of her present hilarity. She is dressed in a tortoise-shell suit, and I know that you will delight in her.

17 November

'All right,' said the Cat; and this time it vanished quite slowly, beginning with the end of the tail, and ending with the grin, which remained some time after the rest of it had gone.

'Well! I've often seen a cat without a grin,' thought Alice; 'but a grin without a cat! It's the most curious thing I ever saw in my life!'

– Lewis Carroll, Alice's *Adventures in Wonderland*

18 November

Today marks Margaret Atwood's birthday; the prize-winning Canadian writer was born on this day in 1939. Here, she muses on her decision to get two new cats.

I have put myself on a list for two Siberian kittens. [...] These will be indoor cats, and trained to walk on a leash, or so I fondly believe. Perhaps I will erect a Catio, so they can sunbathe while watching wildlife safely. I will have cat hammocks. I will have scratching posts. I will not allow myself to be distressed by shredded upholstery.

If I'm going to be a mad old lady with a witchy reputation I may as well equip myself with a couple of trusted familiars. Company as one flies through the air on one's broom, wouldn't you say?

– Margaret Atwood, *An Anthology: On Cats*

19 November

Another moment with Margaret Atwood.

'I was a cat-deprived young child. I longed for a kitten, but was denied one.'

– Margaret Atwood

20 November

The vote was taken at once, and it was agreed by an overwhelming majority that rats were comrades. There were only four dissentients, the three dogs and the cat, who was afterwards discovered to have voted on both sides.

– George Orwell, *Animal Farm*

21 November

Japanese poet and writer Takashi Hiraide was born on this day in 1950. Today's cat is Chibi – 'a jewel of a cat' – the star of his bestselling book *The Guest Cat*.

For me, Chibi is a friend with whom I share an understanding, and who just happens to have taken on the form of a cat.

22 November

Mary Ann Evans, better known as George Eliot, was born on this day in 1819. To mark her birthday, here's a passage from her first novel, *Adam Bede*. It features a metaphorical rather than a literal literary cat, as Mr and Mrs Poyser speculate on a romantic attachment between the titular Adam Bede and Dinah Morris.

'Hey-day! There's Adam along wi' Dinah,' said Mr. Poyser, as he opened the far gate into the Home Close. 'I couldna think how he happened away from church. Why,' added good Martin, after a moment's pause, 'what dost think has just jumped into my head?'

'Summat as hadna far to jump, for it's just under our nose. You mean as Adam's fond o' Dinah.'

'Aye! hast ever had any notion of it before?'

'To be sure I have,' said Mrs. Poyser, who always declined, if possible, to be taken by surprise. 'I'm not one o' those as can see the cat i' the dairy an' wonder what she's come after.'

23 November

I thought, shivering, that there are things that outweigh comfort, unless one is an old woman or a cat.
– Ursula K Le Guin, *The Left Hand of Darkness*

24 November

Agnes Grey by Anne Brontë was published on this day in 1847. As we've seen, the Brontë sisters were dedicated cat-lovers, so it's no surprise when a feline's whiskered face pops up within the pages of their books.

My dear little friend, the kitten, would certainly be changed; she was already growing [into] a fine cat; and when I returned, even for a hasty visit at Christmas, would, most likely, have forgotten both her playmate and her merry pranks. I had romped with her for the last time; and when I stroked her soft bright fur, while she lay purring herself to sleep in my lap, it was with a feeling of sadness I could not easily disguise.

25 November

On this day in 1943, Ernest Hemingway wrote a letter to his first wife Hadley in which he described the many cats who shared his home in Cuba. (See 21 July for more on Hemingway's cats.)

In case you are in hospital or in bed and want to be amused or informed, let's say, there are eleven cats here. One cat just leads to another. The mother is Tester, a Persian from the Silver Dawn Cattery somewhere in Florida. She had a kitten named Thruster out of Dillinger, a black and white cat from Cojimar, a coastal fishing village. By the same sir she also bore Furhouse, Fats, Friendless and Friendless's Brother. All in the same litter [...] We also have a grey, sort of snow leopard cat named Uncle Wolfer (Persian) and a Tiger cat from Guanabacoa named Good Will after Nelson Rockerfeller. There are at present two half grown kittens named Blindie [...] and Nuisance Value also known as Littless Kitty, who is the most beautiful of all with a purr-purr that would blast you out of the hospital.

26 November

On this day in 1887, the literary world lost a shining star in the form of Foss, the beloved pet tabby cat of poet Edward Lear. Lear adored Foss, who frequently featured in his drawings and writings, and is thought to have been the inspiration for 'The Owl and the Pussy-cat' (see 12 May). This rather rotund and stumpy-tailed cat died a few months before Lear himself, and the poet gave him an elaborate funeral. The delightful feline is commemorated in Lear's verse 'Self-Portrait of the Laureate of Nonsense'.

He has many friends, lay men and clerical,
Old Foss is the name of his cat;
His body is perfectly spherical,
He weareth a runcible hat.

27 NOVEMBER

Now all the cats were getting spoogy and running and
jumping in a like cat-panic, and some were blaming
each other, hitting out cat-tolchocks with the old lapa
and ptaaaaa and grrrrr and kraaaaakrk.

– Anthony Burgess, *A Clockwork Orange*

28 NOVEMBER

On this day in 1894, Mark Twain's novel *Pudd'nhead Wilson*
was published.

When there was room on the ledge outside of the pots
and boxes for a cat, the cat was there – in sunny weather
– stretched at full length, asleep and blissful, with her
furry belly to the sun and a paw curved over her nose.
Then that house was complete, and its contentment and
peace were made manifest to the world by this symbol,
whose testimony is infallible. A home without a cat – and
a well-fed, well-petted and properly revered cat – may
be a perfect home, perhaps, but how can it prove title?'

29 November

American novelist Louisa M Alcott was born on this day 1832. In her book *Little Women*, the March family keep cats (see 15 November), and it is when he returns a runaway cat that Jo March meets their neighbour Laurie for the first time. But of all the sisters, the one who loves cats best is gentle Beth.

> Beth had a headache, and lay on the sofa, trying to comfort herself with the cat and three kittens.

❖❖

30 November

Writer Mark Twain was born on this day in 1835. Cats frequently pop up in his work, as we've seen, but he also kept many cats of his own, including Bambino, Buffalo Bill, Soapy Sal and Sinbad – as well as Famine and Pestilence.

DECEMBER

As the year draws to a close, December is a month to spend time with friends and family, perhaps celebrating Christmas or Hannukah, eating delicious food and staying warm indoors. Most of us enter December with the aim of spending as much time as possible in our pyjamas – and why not? For cats, this month is also a time to attack the Christmas tree and hog the cosiest spot on the sofa.

We'll be hanging out with some festive felines this month, including Polar Bear (see 25 December) and Mog (see 22 December), as well as the rather terrifying Jólaköttur (see 24 December).

As well as being a time for celebration, December offers us the opportunity to look back on the year that has passed and reflect on all we've experienced and learned. Hopefully, most of those experiences will have involved cats. And if you've learned nothing else this year, I hope this book has made one thing perfectly clear: cats and books belong together.

1 DECEMBER

In an interview with Alexander Waugh for *Vanity Fair*, legendary writer V S Naipaul shared his thoughts on life, loss and grief. The extract below concerns the death of Naipaul's beloved cat Augustus.

Sir Vidia's breathing seemed a little better than it had been, and I mentioned to him that maybe he had been allergic to Augustus. 'Yes, my doctor suggested that, too, but I told him I would rather have Augustus and wheeze than breathe freely without him.' [...] I asked what it was that made Augustus so special: 'He knew the land and the garden. He recognised the house and everything in it. He knew me. Therefore he cannot be replaced.'

2 December

When you sit close to a cat you know well, and put your hand on him, trying to adjust to the rhythms of his life, so different from yours, sometimes he will lift his head and greet you with a soft sound different from all his other sounds, acknowledging that he knows you are trying to enter his existence.

– Doris Lessing, 'The Old Age of El Magnifico'

3 December

On this day in 1965, the Beatles released their song 'Norwegian Wood'. Just over twenty years later, Haruki Murakami released his novel of the same name.

A white cat maybe six months old decided she liked me and started eating at my place. I called her Seagull. [...] Every day after work I'd eat at a cheap restaurant, wash it down with beer, go home and play with the cat, then sleep like a dead man.

4 December

Poet Rainer Maria Rilke was born on this day in 1875. Today's
cat is the titular feline from his poem 'The Black Cat'.

She seems to hide all looks that have ever fallen
into her, so that, like an audience,
she can look them over, menacing and sullen,
and curl to sleep with them.

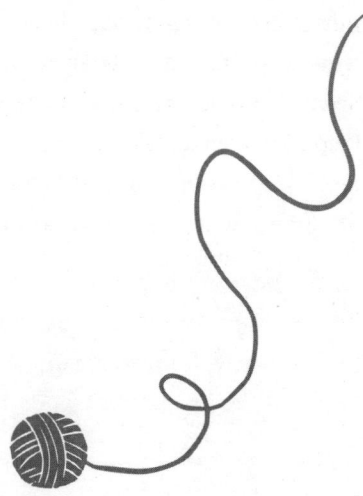

5 December

Poet Christina Rossetti was born on this day in 1830. Perhaps best known for her narrative poem 'Goblin Market', and also for writing the words to 'In the Bleak Midwinter', she also wrote the lament 'On the Death of a Cat, a Friend of Mine, Aged Ten Years and a Half':

Of a noble race she came,
And Grimalkin was her name.
Young and old full many a mouse
Felt the prowess of her house:
Weak and strong full many a rat
Cowered beneath her crushing pat:
And the birds around the place
Shrank from her too close embrace.
But one night, reft of her strength,
She laid down and died at length:
Lay a kitten by her side,
In whose life the mother died.
Spare her line and lineage,
Guard her kitten's tender age,
And that kitten's name as wide
Shall be known as her's that died.

And whoever passes by
The poor grave where Puss doth lie,
Softly, softly, let him tread,
Nor disturb her narrow bed.

In December 2017, a short story was published in the *New Yorker*. 'Cat Person' by Kristen Roupenian quickly went viral, capturing readers' imaginations and becoming something of a cultural phenomenon. It tells the story of a young woman, Margot, who swaps numbers with a man named Robert. They enjoy a flirtation over text, and Margot find herself warming to him – but when they meet for a date in person, things feel very different.

> She learned that Robert had two cats, named Mu and Yan, and together they invented a complicated scenario in which her childhood cat, Pita, would send flirtatious texts to Yan, but whenever Pita talked to Mu she was formal and cold, because she was jealous of Mu's relationship with Yan.

7 December

The cat joined the Re-education Committee and was very active in it for some days. She was seen one day sitting on a roof and talking to some sparrows who were just out of her reach. She was telling them that all animals were now comrades and that any sparrow who chose could come and perch on her paw; but the sparrows kept their distance.

– George Orwell, *Animal Farm*

8 December

When he heard people with no knowledge of a cat's character saying that cats were not as loving as dogs, that they were cold and selfish, he always thought to himself how impossible it was to understand the charm and lovableness of a cat if one had not, like him, spent many years living alone with one. The reason was that all cats are to some extent shy creatures: they won't show affection or seek it from their owners in front of a third person but tend rather to be oddly standoffish. Lily too would ignore Shozo or run off when he called her, if his mother were present. But when the two of them were alone, she would climb up on his lap without being called and devote the most flattering attention to him.

– Jun'ichirō Tanizaki, *A Cat, A Man, and Two Women*

9 December

Japanese novelist Natsume Sōseki died on this day in 1916. Today's cat is the unnamed feline narrator of his novel *I Am a Cat*, who shares his observations about the family he lives with and their friends and neighbours.

> Compared with such complexities, cats are simple. If we want to eat, we eat; if we want to sleep, we sleep; when we are angry, we are angry utterly; when we cry, we cry with all the desperation of extreme commitment to our grief. Thus we never keep things like diaries. For what would be the point? [...] We live our diaries, and consequently have no need to keep a daily record as a means of maintaining our real characters. Had I the time to keep a diary, I'd use that time to better effect; sleeping on the veranda.

10 December

American poet Emily Dickinson was born on this day in 1830. We'll be hearing from her again later this month, but for now here is a brief extract from a letter she wrote to her brother in 1851, perfect for a cosy winter morning spent with a cat.

> The breakfast is warm, and pussy is here a-singing, and the tea kettle sings too, as if to see which was loudest, and I am so afraid lest kitty should be beaten.
>
> – *The Letters of Emily Dickinson*

11 December

As we move deeper into December, party season is upon us, and it seems like the perfect time to revisit our friend Behemoth. Although the scene below doesn't technically take place at a party, he is swinging from a chandelier – and one could argue that wherever Behemoth is, a party is likely to follow.

[T]he cat had contrived to leap through the air and jump up onto the chandelier hanging in the centre of the room.

'A stepladder!' came the cry from below.

'I challenge you to a duel!' yelled the cat, flying over their heads on the swinging chandelier, and at this point the Browning proved to be in his paws again [...] The cat took aim and, flying like a pendulum over the heads of the visitors, he opened fire on them.

– Mikhail Bulgakov, *The Master and Margarita*

12 December

Today's cat is none other than T S Eliot's 'Macavity: The Mystery Cat'.

Macavity, Macavity, there's no one like Macavity,
He's broken every human law, he breaks the laws of gravity.

13 December

We're sticking with T S Eliot today. In a letter from December 1936, Eliot wrote to Polly Tandy with this piece of wisdom:

> When a Cat adopts you, and I am not superstitious at all I don't mean only Black cats there is nothing to be done about it except to put up with it and wait until the wind changes.
>
> – *The Letters of T. S. Eliot, Volume 8: 1936–1938*

14 December

Author Shirley Jackson was born on this day in 1916. Although the narrator of her novel *We Have Always Lived in the Castle* is named Merricat, she is in fact a human girl; it's short for Mary Katherine. Luckily, there is a real cat in the book: Jonas.

> Even Jonas was fretful – he was running up a storm, our mother used to say – and could not sleep quietly; all during those days when the change was coming Jonas stayed restless. From a deep sleep he would start suddenly, lifting his head as though listening, and then, on his feet and moving in one quick ripple, he ran up the stairs and across the beds and around through the doors in and out and then down the stairs and across the hall and over the chair in the dining room and around the table and through the kitchen and out into the garden where he would slow, sauntering, and then pause to lick a paw and flick an ear and take a look at the day. At night we could hear him running, feel him cross our feet as we lay in bed, running up a storm.

15 December

It's panto season in the UK, so today's cat is the feline companion of Dick Whittington from the English folktale 'Dick Whittington and his Cat'. There are many versions of the story, but in most, Whittington's cat is a talented catcher of rodents, and her skill in this area is what first sets him on the path to riches.

And he turned – so cheered he was at that –
And, meeting a boy who carried a cat,
He bought the cat with his only penny,
For where he had slept the mice were many.
Back to the merchant's his way he took,
To the pans and potatoes and cruel cook,
And he found Miss Puss a fine device,
For she kept his garret clear of mice.

16 December

Jane Austen was born on this day in 1775. Cats don't make regular appearances in her novels, but her 1811 work *Sense and Sensibility* does gift us the remark below, when Mrs Jennings talks to Colonel Brandon about Elinor and Marianne Dashwood:

> 'Ah! Colonel, I do not know what you and I shall do without the Miss Dashwoods [...] Lord! we shall sit and gape at one another as dull as two cats.'

17 December

English novelist Dorothy Sayers died on this day in 1957. There is a statue of her in Witham in Essex, UK, where she lived for many years. Standing alongside her, immortalized in bronze, is the figure of her cat, Blitz.

18 December

But a family cat is not just a beautiful thing – as I learnt, over the years. Cats are made of fur because fur absorbs secrets. You can cry into fur. Fur, draped across the heart, will opiate your melancholy. Fur will make you happy again.

– Caitlin Moran, 'A Death in the Family'

19 DECEMBER

How you behave toward cats here below determines
your status in Heaven.

– Robert A Heinlein, *To Sail Beyond the Sunset*

20 DECEMBER

How neatly a cat sleeps,
sleeps with its paws and its posture,
sleeps with its wicked claws...

– Pablo Neruda, 'Cat's Dream'

21 DECEMBER

As Christmas approaches, enjoy this cat-centric description
of a perfect Christmas from a letter written by poet Emily
Dickinson in 1874.

Atmospherically it was the most beautiful Christmas on
record. The hens came to the door with Santa Claus, the
pussies washed themselves in the open air without chilling
their tongues, and Santa Claus – sweet old gentleman –
was even gallanter than usual. [...] Maggie gave the hens a
check for potatoes, each of the cats had a gilt-edged bone,
and the horse had new blankets from Boston.

– *The Letters of Emily Dickinson*

22 December

Today's cat is Mog, the creation of writer and illustrator Judith Kerr (see 14 June). Among this stripy cat's many adventures is *Mog's Christmas*, published in 1976. The charming picture book depicts Mog's confusion as her owners begin busily preparing for Christmas, bringing a tree inside and hanging up holly. When 'white things' fall out of the sky, things get even worse (and rather chilly). As always, though, Mog is happy in the end.

23 December

Today's cat is Mowzer, from the beloved children's book *The Mousehole Cat*, written by Antonia Barber and beautifully illustrated by Nicola Bayley. The book tells the story of 'Old Tom', a fisherman from the Cornish village of Mousehole, who sets out in the midst of a fierce storm to try and catch enough fish to feed his hungry village. The story is based on a local legend about a fisherman named Tom Bawcock, and every year on this day the people of Mousehole celebrate Tom Bawcock's Eve. In the book, Mowzer accompanies Tom on his perilous quest. The storm is personified as a huge cat, and Mowzer uses her purring to calm it enough to allow Tom's boat to return safely.

24 December

Today is Christmas Eve, and our cat is the Jólaköttur (Yule Cat) of Icelandic folklore. The Yule Cat is an enormous feline said to stalk the countryside at this time of year, eating anyone who does not receive new clothing before Christmas Eve.

A good reason to put on your best new outfit!

25 December

Today is Christmas Day, and our festive cat is Cleveland Amory's Polar Bear, whom we first met on 2 September. Here, the feline finds himself face to face with his first Christmas tree.

In the living room I had a modest Christmas tree. Granted, it was not a very big tree – he was not, at that time, a very big cat. Granted, too, that this tree had a respectable pile of gaily wrapped packages around the base and even an animal figure attached to the top. Granted even that it was festooned with lights which, at rhythmic intervals, flashed on and off. To any cat, however, a tree is a tree and this tree, crazed as he was, was no exception. With one bound he cleared the boxes, flashed up through the branches, the lights, and the light cord and managed, somewhere near the top, to disappear again.

– Cleveland Amory, *The Cat Who Came for Christmas*

26 December

English poet Thomas Gray was born on this day in 1716. To mark his birthday, here are some lines from his lament 'Ode on the Death of a Favourite Cat Drowned in a Tub of Goldfishes':

> Her conscious tail her joy declared;
> The fair round face, the snowy beard,
> The velvet of her paws,
> Her coat, that with the tortoise vies,
> Her ears of jet, and emerald eyes,
> She saw; and purred applause.

Sadly, as the poem's title suggests, it ends with the cat meeting her end in the large blue and white bowl of water after trying to catch a little snack:

> She stretched in vain to reach the prize.
> What female hart can gold despise?
> What cat's averse to fish?

27 December

On this day in 1821, Lady Wilde was born. The mother of Oscar Wilde, she was a gifted writer herself, and her work often focused on Irish folktales. One such tale is 'Seanchan the Bard and the King of the Cats', in which the titular bard enrages the king of the cats by satirising him:

'...I shall satirise the tribe of the cats, and their chief lord, Irusan, son of Arusan; for I know where he lives with his wife Spit-fire, and his daughter Sharp-tooth, with her brothers the Purrer and the Growler. But I shall begin with Irusan himself for he is king, and answerable for all the cats.'

And he said, 'Irusan, monster of claws, who strikes at the mouse but lets it go; weakest of cats. The otter did well who bit off the tips of thy progenitor's ears, so that every cat since is jagged-eared. Let thy tail hang down; it is right, for the mouse jeers at thee.'

No wonder Irusan was annoyed.

28 December

Since I got a cat of my own, my life has been full of cats.
– Robertson Davies, *The Diary of Samuel Marchbanks*

29 December

Today is the birthday of David McKean, renowned illustrator of S F Said's children's novel *Varjak Paw*. Today's cat is Varjak, protagonist of the book: a young Mesopotamian Blue who must learn 'the Way of Jalal', a set of skills needed to defeat his enemies.

'There are Seven Skills in the Way of Jalal,' whispered the Elder Paw. His breath was warm in the cold night air. 'We know only three of them. Their names are these: Slow-Time. Moving Circles. Shadow-Walking.' He recited these Skills slowly, in rhythm, like poetry. 'Learn these words, and pass them on in turn.'

30 December

Writer Rudyard Kipling was born on this day in 1865. In his honour, today's cat is none other than the hero of his *Just So* story 'The Cat That Walked by Himself', which explains how the tame animals – the Dog, the Horse, the Cow, the Pig, the Sheep and the Cat – were once wild, 'and they walked in the Wet Wild Woods by their wild lones'.

The Man and the Woman set up a comfortable home in a cave, and the Woman sets about making bargains with the animals – the Dog will get a bone if he helps the Man to hunt; the Cow will be fed grass if it gives milk – but the Cat strikes his own deal, ensuring that he will always be given a bowl of milk and a place to lie by the fire, but will remain free to come and go as he pleases.

I am the Cat who walks by himself, and all places are alike to me.

31 DECEMBER

As we reach the end of the year, let's finish with these words of wisdom from the inimitable Muriel Spark, on the undeniably important role cats play in the worlds of literature and creativity.

[I]f you want to concentrate deeply on some problem, and especially some piece of writing or paper-work, you should acquire a cat. Alone with the cat in the room where you work...the cat will invariably get up on your desk and settle placidly under the desk lamp...The cat will settle down and be serene, with a serenity that passes all understanding. And the tranquillity of the cat will gradually come to affect you, sitting there at your desk, so that all the excitable qualities that impede your concentration compose themselves and give your mind back the self-command it has lost. You need not watch the cat all the time. Its presence alone is enough. The effect of a cat on your concentration is remarkable, very mysterious.

– Muriel Spark, *A Far Cry from Kensington*

REFERENCES

'Dorothy L Sayers'. Public Statues and Sculpture Association (PSSA).

'Monsieur Dumas and his Beasts'. In: *The Animal Story Book*, edited by Andrew Lang. Longmans, Green & Co, 10904.

'Proust Questionnaire: Edward Gorey'. Vanity Fair, October 1997.

Adams, Douglas, and Carwardine, Mark. *Last Chance to See.* Cornerstone, 2013.

Adams, Douglas. *The Restaurant at the End of the Universe.* Macmillan Children's, 2010.

Adams, Richard. *Watership Down.* Simon and Schuster, 2009.

Alexander, Lloyd. *Time Cat.* Square Fish, 2012.

Amory, Cleveland. *The Cat Who Came for Christmas.* Back Bay Books, 2013.

Appelt, Kathi. *The Underneath.* Atheneum, 2010.

Arikawa, Hiro. *The Travelling Cat Chronicles.* Random House, 2017.

Asimov, Isaac (writing as George E Dale). 'Time Pussy'. In *Astounding Science-Fiction*, edited by John W Campbell and Catherine Tarrant. Vol. XXIX, No. 2, April 1942.

Atwood, Margaret. 'Introduction'. In: *On Cats: An Anthology.* Notting Hill Editions, 2021

Backman, Fredrick. *A Man Called Ove.* Thorndike, 2014.

Barbery, Muriel. *The Elegance of the Hedgehog.* Europa Editions, 2008.

Baudelaire, Charles. 'Cat'. Les Fleurs Du Mal: *The Complete Text of the Flowers of Evil*, translated by Richard Howard. David R Godine Publisher, 1982.

Benson, Margaret. *The Soul of a Cat and Other Stories.* William Heinemann, 1901.

Blume, Judy. S*tarring Sally J. Freedman As Herself.* Simon and Schuster, 2000.

Boswell, James. *The Life of Samuel Johnson.* Penguin, 2008.

Bowen, James. *A Street Cat Named Bob.* Hodder & Stoughton, 2012.

Bradbury, Ray. 'The Cat's Pajamas'. In: *The Cat's Pajamas: Stories.* Harper Collins, 2004.

Brockes, Emma. Quoted in: 'Haruki Murakami: 'I took a gamble and survived." Guardian, 14 October 2011.

Brooke, Rupert. *Letters from America.* McClelland, Goodchild & Stewart, 1916.

Bukowski, Charles. Letter to Carl Weissner, November 1966. *Screams from the Balcony: Selected Letters 1960–1970.* Harper Collins, 2007.

Bukowski, Charles. Letter to Neeli Cherry, April 1963. *Screams from the Balcony: Selected Letters 1960–1970.* Harper Collins, 2007

Bulgakov, Mikhail. *The Master and Margarita*. Alma, 2020.

Burgess, Anthony. *A Clockwork Orange*. Ballantine Books, 1988.

Burroughs, William S. *The Cat Inside*. Penguin, 2009.

Burton, Jessie. 'Book clinic: Can you recommend novels and nonfiction books about cats?'. Guardian, 10 August 2019.

Cabot, Meg. *The Princess Diaries*. Pan Macmillan, 2015.

Camus, Albert. *A Happy Death*. Penguin Classics, 2013.

Camuti, Louis J and Alexander, Lloyd. Park Avenue Vet. Holt, Rhinehart and Winston, 1962.

Capote, Truman. *Breakfast at Tiffany's*. Penguin, 1961.

Carter, Angela. 'Puss in Boots'. *The Bloody Chamber and Other Stories*. Random House, 1995.

Chandler, Raymond. Letter to Charles Morton, March 1945. 'Am I really writing it at all?' Letters of Note.

Christie, Agatha. *A Murder is Announced*. Harper Collins, 2010.

Clarke, Susanne. *Jonathan Strange & Mr Norrell*. A&C Black, 2005.

Cleary, Beverly. *Socks*. Harper Collins, 2015.

Colette. *Chance Acquaintances and Julie De Carneilhan*. Vintage Classics 2001.

Colette. *The Cat*. In: *Six Novels: Colette*. Stoddart, 1988.

Collins, Suzanne. *The Hunger Games*. Scholastic, 2014.

Cooper, Gwen. *Homer's Odyssey*. Delacorte Press, 2009.

Dahl, Roald. 'Edward the Conqueror'. In: *The Roald Dahl Omnibus*. Barnes & Noble, 1993.

Davies, Robertson. *The Diary of Samuel Marchbanks*. Clarke, Irwin, 1947.

Davies, W H 'The Cat'. *The Song of Life and Other Poems*. Cornell University Library, 2009.

de Beauvoir, Simone. Quoted in: Ward, Julie K. 'Reciprocity and Friendship in Beauvoir's Thought'. Hypatia, Vol. 14, No. 4, Autumn 1999, pp36–49.

Dickinson, Emily. *The Complete Poems of Emily Dickinson*, edited by Thomas H Johnson. Faver & Faber, 2016

Dickinson, Emily. *The Letters of Emily Dickinson*, edited by Mabel Loomis Todd. Roberts Brothers, 1894.

Donne, John. 'VI. Meditation: The physician is afraid'. *Devotions Upon Emergent Occasions (together with Death's Duel)*. Ann Arbor Paperbacks, 1959.

Dunne, Nora. Quoted in: 'Joyce Carol Oates makes them laugh, makes them squirm, in Boston'. *Christian Science Monitor*, 18 October 2010.

Eliot, George. *Adam Bede*. Wordsworth Editions, 1997.

Eliot, T S 'Bustopher Jones'. *Old Possum's Book of Practical Cats*. Faber & Faber, 1939.

Eliot, T S 'Macavity: The Mystery Cat'. *Old Possum's Book of Practical Cats*. Faber & Faber, 1939.

Eliot, T S 'The Rum Tum Tugger'. Old Possum's Book of Practical Cats. Faber & Faber, 1939.

Eliot, T S Letter to Polly Tandy, December 1936. *The Letters of T. S. Eliot, Volume 8: 1936–1938*. Faber & Faber 2019.

Enright, Anne. *The Gathering*. Vintage, 2011.

Estés, Clarissa Pinkola. *Women Who Run With the Wolves*. Rider, 2022.

Eugenides, Jeffrey. *The Virgin Suicides*. Warner Books, 1994.

Ewart, Gavin. 'A 14 year old convalescent cat in the winter'. In: T*he Nations Favourite Twentieth Century Poems*, edited by Griff Rhys Jones. BBC Books/Random House, 1999.

Farjeon, Eleanor. *Faithful Jenny Dove and Other Tales*. Books for Libraries Press, 1970.

Filipovíc, Emir. Quoted in: Nuwer, Rachel. 'Centuries ago, a cat walked across this medieval manuscript'. *Smithsonian Magazine*, 12 March 2013.

Finn, A J. *The Woman in the Window*. Harper Collins, 2018.

Fitzgerald, Zelda. *Save Me the Waltz*. Arcturus Books, 1967.

Fleischer, Leonore. *The Cat's Pajamas*. Harper & Row, 1982.

Flood, Alison. Quoted in: 'Charles Bukowski's book on cats to show his gentler side.' *Guardian*, 24 March 2015.

Flynn, Gillian. *Gone Girl*. Crown Publishers, 2012.

Gallico, Paul. *Honorable Cat*. Crown Publishing Group, 1972.

Gallico, Paul. *Thomasina, the Cat Who Thought She Was God*. Doubleday, 2007.

García Márquez, Gabriel. *Love in the Time of Cholera*. Penguin, 1989.

Ginsberg, Allen. Letter to Jack Kerouac, 9 November 1954. *The Letters of Allen Ginsberg*, edited by Bill Morgan. De Capo, 2008.

Grant, Rob and Naylor, Doug. *Red Dwarf: Infinity Welcomes Careful Drivers*. Roc, 1989.

Haig, Matt. *The Midnight Library*. Canongate, 2021.

Hall, Steven. *The Raw Shark Texts*. Canongate, 2007.

Hamerton, Philip Gilbert. *Chapters on Animals*. Roberts Brothers, 1884.

Harris, Joanne. *Chocolat*. Doubleday, 1999.

Hearn, Lafcadio. 'The Boy Who Drew Cats'. In: *The Boy Who Drew Cats and other Japanese Fairy Tales*. Dover Children's Thrift Classics, 2012.

Heilpern, John. *Conference of the Birds: The Story of Peter Brook in Africa*. Routledge, 1999.

Heinlein, Robert A. *The Cat Who Walks Through Walls*. Ace Books, 1988.

Heinlein, Robert A. *The Door Into Summer*. Doubleday, 1957.

Heinlein, Robert A. *To Sail Beyond the Sunset*. Ace Books 1988.

Heller, Zoë. *Notes on a Scandal*. Penguin, 2004.

Herford, Oliver. Quoted in: *The Reader's Digest*, vol 121. 1982.

Herriot, James. *Cat Stories*. McClelland & Stewart, 1994.

Highsmith, Patricia. 'Ming's Biggest Prey'. In: *Mystery Cats: Felonious Felines from Ellery Queen's Mystery Magazine and Alfred Hitchcock's Mystery Magazine*. G K Hall, 1994.

Hoffman, Alice. *Practical Magic*. Scribner, 2017.

Holland, Barbara. *The Secrets of the Cat*. Ballantine Books, 1989.

Holman, John. *Luminous Mysteries*. Harcourt Brace, 1998.

Hornby, Nick. *High Fidelity*. Penguin, 2000.

Hoshino, Tomoyuki. 'We, the Children of Cats'. In: *We, the Children of Cats: Stories and Novellas*, translated by Brian Bergstrom. PM Press, 2012.

Howe, James and Deborah. Bunnicula. In: *The Bunnicula Collection*. Atheneum, 1999.

Huxley, Aldous. 'Sermons in Cats'. *Vanity Fair*, September 1930.

Ishida, Syou. *We'll Prescribe You a Cat*. Translated by E. Madison Shimoda. Doubleday, 2024.

Jackson Braun, Lilian. *The Cat Who Could Read Backwards*. Compass Press, 1997.

Jackson, Shirley. *We Have Always Lived in the Castle*. Penguin, 1984.

Jacques, Brian. *Mossflower*. Avon Books, 1990.

Jansson, Tove. *The Summer Book*. Translated by Thomas Teal. G K Hall, 1977.

Jarvis, Robin. *The Dark Portal* (The Deptford Mice). Pushkin Press, 2024.

Joseph, Michael. *Cat's Company*. Geoffrey Bles, 1930.

Joyce, James. *Ulysses*. Oxford University Press, 1998.

Kawamura, Genki. *If Cats Disappeared from the World*. Pan Macmillan, 2018.

Kerouac, Jack. *Big Sur*. Penguin, 1992.

Kerr, Judith. *Mog's Christmas*. Harper Collins, 2020.

King, Stephen. 'L T's Theory of Pets'. In: *Everything's Eventual*. Simon & Schuster, 2002.

King, Stephen. 'The Cat from Hell'. *Just After Sunset*. Scribner, 2008.

King, Stephen. *Doctor Sleep*. Hodder & Stoughton, 2013.

King, Stephen. *Pet Sematary*. Simon & Schuster, 2002.

King, Stephen. *Under the Dome*. Hodder & Stoughton, 2009.

Krutch, Joseph Wood. *Henry David Thoreau*. William Sloane Associates, 1948.

Lankester Brisley, Joyce. *Milly-Molly-Mandy Stories*. Puffin Books, 1972.

Lardner, Ring. 'It Looks Bad for the Three Little Lardner Kittens (1922)'. In: *On Cats: An Anthology*. Notting Hill Editions, 2021

Le Guin, Ursula K. '114. My Life So Far, by Pard (Part i): The Annals of Pard XIX'. ursulakleguin.com, 2 May 2016.

Le Guin, Ursula K. 'Schrödinger's Cat'. In: *Universe 5*, edited by Terry Carr. Random House, 1974.

Le Guin, Ursula K. *The Lathe of Heaven*. Simon & Schuster, 1999.

Le Guin, Ursula K. *The Left Hand of Darkness*. Penguin, 1987.

Lessing, Doris. 'An Old Woman and Her Cat'. *The Temptation of Jack Orkney: Collected Stories Volume 2*. Flamingo, 2002.

Lessing, Doris. 'Rufus the Survivor'. In: *On Cats*. Harper Perennial, 2008.

Lessing, Doris. 'The Old Age of El Magnifico'. In: *On Cats*. Harper Perennial, 2008.

Lessing, Doris. Particularly Cats. In: *On Cats*. Harper Perennial, 2008.

Lewis, C S *The Last Battle*. Index Books, 2003.

Lewis, C S *The Lion, the Witch and the Wardrobe*. Harper Collins, 2009.

Lidz, Gogo. 'Soon you too can tour Hunter S Thompson's house'. *Newsweek Magazine*, 15 July 2015.

Lockwood, Patricia. *No One is Talking About This*. Riverhead, 2021.

Lorenz, Konrad. *Man Meets Dog*. Psychology Press, 2002.

Lovecraft, H P 'Nietzscheism and Realism'. *Collected Essays, Volume 5: Philosophy*, edited by S T Joshi. Hippocampus Press, 2006.

Lovecraft, H P 'The Cats of Ulthar'. In: *The Complete Tales of H P Lovecraft*. Rock Point, 2019.

MacKenzie, Victoria. F*or Thy Great Pain Have Mercy on My Little Pain*. Bloomsbury, 2023.

Mantel, Hilary. *Wolf Hall*. Henry Holt, 2009.

Marquis, Don. *Archy and Mehitabel*. Dolphin Books, 1930.

Martel, Yann. *Life of Pi*. Canongate, 2001.

Martin, George R R *A Feast for Crows*. Harper Voyager, 2011.

McEwan, Ian. *The Daydreamer*. Harper Trophy, 1994.

Meissner, Susan. *As Bright As Heaven*. Berkley, 2018.

Méry, Fernand. *The Life, History and Magic of the Cat*. Grosset & Dunlap, 1968.

Michaels, Barbara. *Vanish with the Rose*. Simon & Schuster, 1992.

Mitchell, Margaret. *Gone with the Wind*. Pocket Books, 2008.

Mochizuki, Mai. *The Full Moon Coffee Shop*. Translated by Jesse Kirkwood. Brazen, 2024.

Moran, Caitlin. 'A Death in the Family'. *The Times*, 25 March 2017.

Moray Williams, Ursula. *Gobbolino the Witch's Cat*. Puffin, 2014.

Morris, Desmond. *Catwatching*. Ebury 2002.

Morrow Lindbergh, Anne. *Listen! The Wind*. Harcourt, Brace, 1938.

Murakami, Haruki. *Kafka on the Shore*. Alfred A. Knopf, 2002.

Murakami, Haruki. *Norwegian Wood*. Vintage, 2003.

Murakami, Haruki. *The Wind-Up Bird Chronicle*. Vintage, 1999.

Murakami, Huraki. *IQ84*. Random House, 2011.

Murdoch, Iris. *The Nice and the Good*. Random House, 2000.

Murphy, Jill. The Worst Witch. In: *The Worst Witch at School*. Candlewick, 2007.

Naylor, Phyllis Reynolds. *Shiloh*. Atheneum, 2000.

Niffenegger, Audrey, 'Secret Life, With Cats', In: *Ghostly: A Collection of Ghost Stories*, edited by Audrey Niffenegger. Random House, 2015.

Nix, Garth. *Lirael*. Hot Key, 2014.

O'Brien, Robert C. *Mrs Frisby and the Rats of NIMH*. Puffin, 2014.

O'Connor, Flannery. 'A Good Man is Hard to Find'. In: *A Good Man is Hard to Find, and Other Stories*. Harcourt Brace, 1981.

Oates, Joyce Carol. 'The White Cat'. *Narrative Magazine*.

Orwell, George. *Animal Farm*. Little, Brown, 2021.

Paul, Pamela. Quoted in: 'The saying goes: Dogs are a man's best friend. But cats are better'. *New York Times*.

Peake, Mervyn. *Titus Groan. The Gormenghast Trilogy*. Vintage, 1999.

Peters, Elizabeth. *Seeing a Large Cat*. Hachette, 2012.

Plath, Sylvia. 'Ella Mason and Her Eleven Cats'. *Collected Poems*. Faber & Faber, 1981.

Plath, Sylvia. 'Lady Lazarus'. *Collected Poems*. Faber and Faber, 1981.

Pratchett, Terry. *Lords and Ladies*. Random House, 2013.

Pratchett, Terry. *Men at Arms*. Corgi, 1994.

Pratchett, Terry. *The Amazing Maurice and His Educated Rodents*. Harper Collins, 2008.

Pratchett, Terry. *The Unadulterated Cat*. Gollancz, 1989.

Pratchett, Terry. *Wintersmith*. Corgi Childrens, 2014.

Pratchett, Terry. *Witches Abroad*. Corgi, 1992.

Pullman, Philip. *The Subtle Knife*. Scholastic, 1997.

Reid Banks, Lynne. *Return of the Indian*. Harper Collins, 2003.

Repplier, Agnes. *The Fireside Sphinx*. Riverside Press, 1901.

Rice, Anne. *Interview with the Vampire*. Knopf, 2007.

Roethke, Theodore. 'Praise to the End! [Poem].' *The Sewanee Review* 58, no. 1 (1950):

Roupenian, Kristen. 'Cat Person'. *New Yorker*, 11 December 2017.

Rundell, Katherine. *Super-Infinite: The Transformations of John Donne*. Faber, 2022.
Nicholson, Catherine. Quoted in: 'Batter My Heart'. *London Review of Books*, Vol. 45, No. 2, 19 January 2023.

Said, S F. *Varjak Paw*. David Flicking Books, 2003.

Scannell, Vernon. *How to Enjoy Poetry*. Piatkus, 1987.

Schultz, Colin. Quoted in: 'Ernest Hemingway taught one of his many, many cats to drink whisky'. *Smithsonian Magazine*, 25 September 2013.

Schwab, V E. *The Invisible Life of Addie La Rue*. Titan, 2023.

Shelley, Percy. *Letters: Shelley in Italy*. Clarendon Press, 1964.

Sitwell, Edith. Quoted in: 'Edith Sitwell', National Portrait Gallery.

Sleigh, Barbara. *Carbonel*. Puffin, 2015.

Smart, Christopher. *Jubilate Agno*. Harvard University Press, 1954.

Smith, Ali. *Winter*. Hamish Hamilton, 2017.

Smith, Stevie. 'The Singing Cat'. In: *The Nation's Favourite Twentieth Century Poems*, edited by Griff Rhys Jones. BBC Books/Random House, 1999.

Smith, Zadie. *White Teeth*. Hamish Hamilton, 2000.

Soden, Oliver. *Jeoffry: The Poet's Cat*. History Press, 2020.

Södergran, Edith. *Love & Solitude: Selected Poems, 1916–1923*. Fjord Press, 1992.

Sōseki, Natsume. *I Am a Cat*, translated by Aiko Itō and Graeme Wilson. Rutland, 1972.

Spark, Muriel. *A Far Cry From Kensington*. Viking, 1988.

Sparks, Muriel. *Robinson*. New Directions Publishing, 2003.

Steinbeck, John. *The Winter of our Discontent*. Penguin, 2001.

Steinem, Gloria. Quoted in: Nastasi, Alison. *Writers and their Cats*. Chronicle, 2018.

Summers, Hal. 'My Old Cat'. In: *The Nation's Favourite Twentieth Century Poems*, edited by

Griff Rhys Jones. BBC Books/Random House, 1999.

Tangye, Derek. *A Cat in the Window: Tales from a Cornish Flower Farm*. Constable & Robinson, 2014.

Tanizaki, Jun'ichirō. *A Cat, a Man, and Two Women*. New Directions, 2015.

Tesla, Nikola. 'A Story of Youth Told By Age: Dedicated to Miss Pola Fotitch'.

Thoreau, Henry David. *The Writings of Henry David Thoreau: Journal*, Ed. by B Torrey, 1832–1846, 1850–Nov. 3, 1861. HardPress, 2019.

Tolkien, J R R *The Hobbit*. Ballantine, 1973.

Tolkien, J R R *The Lord of the Rings*. Harper Collins, 1993.

Twain, Mark. *Mark Twain's Notebook*, edited by Albert Bigelow Paine. Harper & Brothers, 1935.

Twain, Mark. Quoted in: *Who is Mark Twain*, edited by Robert H Hirst. Harper Collins, 2009.

Twain, Mark. *Roughing It*. University of California Press, 2011.

Ward, Catriona. *The Last House on Needless Street*. Viper, 2021.

Waugh, Alexander. 'Good style should be imperceptible': V S Naipaul's Lessons on Life, Literature, and Being Left Alone.' *Vanity Fair*, 16 August 2018.

Wells, H G. *The Invisible Man*. Penguin, 2012.

Wells, H G. *The World of William Clissold*. Heron Books, 1969.

West, Jessamyn. *A Matter of Time*. Harcourt, Brace & World, 1966.

Williams, Eley. *The Liar's Dictionary*. William Heinemann, 2020.

Williams, Tad. *Tailchaser's Song*. Hodder & Stoughton, 2015.

Williams, William Carlos. 'Poem'. In: *Poetry: A Magazine of Verse*, edited by Harriet Monroe. Vol. XXXVI, No. IV. July 1930.

Wilson, Jacqueline. *The Cat Mummy*. Transworld, 2001.

Winterson, Jeanette. 'The pet I'll never forget: Jeanette Winterson on Silver, 'the brightest cat I ever had''. *Guardian*. 25 December 2023.

Wodehouse, P G. *Mulliner Nights*. Herbert Jenkins, 1933.

Wood Krutch, Joseph. *The Twelve Seasons*. W Sloane Associates, 1949.

Woolf, Virginia. *A Room of One's Own*. Penguin Classics, 2020.

Woolf, Virginia. *Between the Acts*. Harcourt, 1970.

Woolf, Virginia. *The Waves*. Vintage Classics, 2016

Yoder, Rachel. *Nightbitch*. Vintage, 2021.

Zelazny, Roger. *A Night in the Lonesome October*. Chicago Review Press, 2014.

Zola, Émile. 'The Paradise of Cats'. In: *The Complete Works of Émile Zola*. Delphi Classics, 2013.